MW00987603

NECROSCOPE:
THE PLAGUE-BEARER

NECROSCOPE: THE PLAGUE-BEARER

BRIAN LUMLEY

SUBTERRANEAN PRESS 2010

Necroscope: The Plague-Bearer
Copyright © 2010 by Brian Lumley. All rights reserved.

Dust jacket and interior illustrations Copyright © 2010
by Bob Eggleton. All rights reserved.

Interior design Copyright © 2010 by Desert Isle Design, LLC.
All rights reserved.

First Edition

ISBN
978-1-59606-272-6

Subterranean Press
PO Box 190106
Burton, MI 48519

www.subterraneanpress.com

I

Descendants of an ancient line, the brothers Francezci had gone down beneath the labyrinthine cellars and rock-hewn foundations of their ancestral estate, Le Manse Madonie, into a vast cavern in the mountain's heart. Answering a "call" heard in their vampire minds alone, there they now stood at the wall of the dried-out well which, since that time when it had become necessary to lodge their mutated changeling father there, away from the knowledge—and especially the sight—of common men, they had come to call "the pit."

"The pit:" That was how they thought of the Old Ferenczy's well-cell in the roots of Le Manse Madonie, in this cavern forbidden to all men except the Francezcis (once the Ferenczys, in an era when that name had been far less synonymous with horror) who themselves were very much other than men proper, though not to the same degree as their mainly formless metamorph father.

But the Old Ferenczy was safe here—and the brothers safe from him, who was their oracle despite that he had his turns—and all would be in order so long as he remained confined here, contained in the well under the cap of electrified wire-mesh in a circular frame that spanned the yawning darkness like a grill. And down there in the perpetual gloom at a depth of some eighty feet, where the shaft opened into a cyst-like chamber that long ago held water seeping from the dripstone walls, now was housed the brothers' hideous sire—the one who in his way had called them here.

Gazing into the unquiet depths they knew he was there; knew also that *he* knew they had come in answer to his call, and that they now stood at the rim of "the pit."

It is probable that to most men this name—its very *sound*—would conjure visions of the Pit of Hell, but to the Francezci brothers the notion of even *that* pit, the entrance to purgatory itself, could never be possessed of the terror inherent in this one. For it was undeniably real: an almost tangible thing, an emanation issuing from the well in a viscous, mental miasma that clung like slime: their father's telepathic thoughts…

Up above on a comparatively remote plateau, Le Manse Madonie's sprawling, fortress-like structure in its many high-walled acres stood square and flat on the rim of a ravine in the rocky heights over Cefalu, Sicily. In its altitude and appearance the place might be thought of as an aerie; and in fact and in *every* respect it was nothing less than that: an aerial redoubt of the Wamphyri! But with the exception of the brothers Francezci themselves, along with their common vampire servitors and adherents, no one else was aware of that fact.

On the contrary, Le Manse Madonie—for all that it seldom entertained guests—had the reputation of being the retreat of the gentlest of gentlemen; and their presence had been requested, however rarely accepted, at every major social event on the island ever since they had come into their inheritance and possession of Le Manse Madonie. And as for the Francezci bloodline: There had been Francezcis in the manse for as long as men could remember. Noted for its male twins, the family's line went back into the dimmest mists of history—and into some of the blackest—but that last was for the brothers alone to know.

Thus the immemorial connection of the Francezcis with certain of Sicily's—and indeed the world's—less savory elements continued to go unsuspected; or if it was then it wasn't mentioned in polite circles. Yet in their role of freelance intelligence agents for the Mob or mobs—as advisers in the fields of international crime, various kinds of espionage, and terrorism—the Francezcis were an unparalleled success story. Where such intelligence had its source...that too was for the secretive, occasionally reclusive brothers alone to know and for others to guess at. But to the Dons it seemed obvious that they had corrupted the otherwise incorruptible on a worldwide scale.

In fact their power base had its source right here, in the shape, or shapelessness, of the thing in the pit: their precognizant father. And now he had something to impart; something of obvious importance, for he was not the one to waste his efforts in common conversation. And now his thoughts came seething in a burst of mental energy, to drive them back a pace from the pit:

Ah, my sons, my keepers...dear Anthony, and my oh-so-dear *Francesco! But tell me now, what is the meaning of this? Do you cringe? What, the invincible Francezci brothers, shrinking from a harmless old thing in a pit?*

"From the power of your telepathic voice, Father," Anthony, who had been the Old Ferenczy's "favourite" in the years before that one's collapse—his total surrender to the devolution of his flesh, its constant flux and flow, and his descent into the subsequent mental degeneration which had overcome him—finally answered. "Each time we converse in this fashion, it seems your sendings have gained that much more strength. So much that they invariably repel us; at least until we recover from their initial shock."

*Oh? And am I so shocking? Oh, ha-ha-ha! Of course I am. Yet still you care and…*provide *for me. Well, from time to time, when you bring to me the occasional tidbit. For instance, right now? A girl, perhaps? Young, clean, ripe and…full of blood?* (That last coming as a monstrous mental gurgle; which scarcely horrified the brothers, whose vampire appetites were almost the equal of those of the thing in the pit.)

"Not now, Father, no—" Anthony answered, "—but soon, I promise. To which end…do I detect your desire to offer some small incentive? Is there perhaps an item of benefit, knowledge that you might wish to impart?"

Huh! the metamorph replied, however bitterly. *As always I'm required to pay—to beg like a dog—for even the smallest of pleasures! But as that old saying goes, beggars can't be choosers, and such is my lot. Yes, there is a matter to discuss: one of great importance, for I have dreamed a dream.*

"Him and his dreams!" Francesco muttered under his breath, scowling and forgetting if only for a moment that not even his thoughts were safe from the Old Ferenczy, not in close proximity like this. But in the next moment he gave a startled jerk, recoiling once again as the old thing in the pit chastised him, snarling in his mind:

Ah, Francesco! Wretch that you were, and ungrateful wretch that you are! Tell me: What would you have been without me, eh? Without my dreams, knowledge, and advice given unstintingly down all the endless years what would have become of you, eh?

Where would you be hiding now but in the craggy keeps of some foreign land, and your aerie a forgotten, crumbling castle full of bats and spiders? Hah!

"Father!" Anthony got between, physically shoving Francesco aside while warning him to be quiet with a glance from gathered eyebrows. "Father, how can we help but be jealous of your dreaming skills, your oneiromancy, and unfailing fathoming of future events? But you are right: You are the origin and source of all that we have risen to, the *Power* behind our power in the world. Francesco perhaps forgets himself; but he is simply eager, as I myself am eager, to learn of your divinations."

For long moments there was only emptiness, a sullen silence like a mental veil on the psychic ether, which gradually lifted until the pit-thing's thoughts "sounded" again in the brothers' minds: his seething yet simultaneously soothing, partially hypnotic telepathic voice. *Ah, Anthony! My true one! And as always you fend well for a foolish, undeserving sibling!*

"Francesco is my brother, yes," said Anthony, with a small, almost regretful shrug of his shoulders. And then, frowning, he held up a hand to once more caution Francesco against any would be protest. "He is my brother—*and* your true son, a bloodson, no less than I myself. Be gracious and forgive him, Father."

Hmmm! said that one. *Then let him bring me a small tribute, and all will be forgiven.*

"I have promised," said Anthony, with a nod of his head.

But let Francesco deliver the...the gift. The Old Ferenczy's "voice" was thick as phlegm. *And let him attend me here at the well, while I...while I* enjoy *it.*

With a quick glance at his sullen brother, Anthony nodded a second time. "It shall be as you wish."

Let him *tell me it is so.*

And keeping a rein on his furious, volatile thoughts, Francesco answered aloud: "Of course I'll deliver your… *tribute,* Father, as soon as we find a safe, suitable provider."

Good! And now hear me out, both of you, for there are great dangers in the world which must be dealt with, and soon.

And after a pause for thought:

While I have seen tomorrow and tomorrow, the future remains… difficult. I can never see far enough into future time, and as always what I do see may have complications, perhaps because *I see it!*

"The Heisenberg principle," said Anthony, who was well read in such things. "Whatever we study we change."

Indeed, and the future is a devious thing. But I know nothing of this Heisenberg; well, except what I see in your mind. A scientist, you say? But aye, the future has occasionally played me false, even a master dreamer such as myself. Still, it would be foolish not to heed its warnings…

Across the world, fifteen hundred miles and more—in Scotland as it is known today—a dog-Lord slumbers in his mountain lair. You know of which I speak: Radu Lykan, hibernating in his amber trough down all the centuries. While he sleeps, the great hound is not a problem. But Radu has a moon-child guardian, one whose name is also known to you.

"Bonnie Jean Mirlu," Anthony cut in. "A common vampire. And we should have dealt with her before now, but—"

—*An* uncommon *vampire!* His father cut him short. *A werewolf bitch: a moon-child, as stated. She has a pack, all female, but they too are of small concern—so long as Radu sleeps. Ah, but Radu is our enemy, has been our enemy these thousands of years, no less than the Drakuls and their lone survivor. Oh yes, the Drakuls, Lykans, and Ferenczys: enemies since times supposedly immemorial. But ancestral memories will never let it rest. The hatred like the blood runs deep, and I have felt Radu stirring in the resin that preserves him!*

The brothers moved closer, gazed down into the deep throat of the pit, and Francesco said, "He will be up? Radu is awakening? Is that what you're saying?"

Oh, ha-ha-ha! The pit-thing laughed in their minds. *Suddenly I have your attention in full, eh? And what is this I smell: sweat on your flesh, and cold? Do you tremble? And is that fear in your blood, Francesco mine? Can you feel that great hound's fangs gnawing at your throat, tearing you even now? Oh, ha-ha-haaaa!*

The Old Ferenczy's mad laughter slowly faded away, and in a while his "voice" continued to sound, but low and yet more sinister and sibilant now:

*You and them that you control can handle the moon-child and her bitch pack well enough I fancy. But my dreams have shown me someone else: a glimpse, nothing more. A man, someone in thrall to her and under her spell. A stranger. Yesss! And indeed he is a strange one! He has...*talents, *which as yet I cannot fathom. In my dreams he comes and goes...hard to explain. Ah, but one thing is certain: He makes Bonnie Jean's existence so much more dangerous to us, which might well mean that the dog-Lord Radu's future rising—an event which was only a possibility until now—has become a probability.*

In the far past Radu was...oh, he was powerful! *The Drakuls were likewise strong, but they feared Radu. Which is why it behooves us to deal with his guardian moon-child and put an end to the bitch pack that she controls, along with her new champion, who or whatever he may be. As for how this may be achieved: alas that I personally can do nothing. For while my sons are up and about I... must remain down. But through me you have established yourselves in the world. You have resources: your wealth and power, a sufficiency of vampire thralls, and the ability to make more. Wherefore you must devise a scheme to destroy Radu's guardian pack, and when that is accomplished to kill the sleeping dog-Lord himself. Aye, and preferably in his sleep...*

So then, what is your response?

"We have a number of thralls, agents, abroad in the world," said Anthony. "I think we should choose the members of a powerful team and let them deal with the Mirlu woman and her thralls."

No! (The brothers sensed the shake of what passed for their changeling father's head, in whatever shape it was now.) *Do not rely on them who are your agents and informers abroad. They are established—your sleepers in the world—and should be kept that way: hidden, covert. You cannot afford to have them reveal themselves; you will certainly need them in times to come. What is more, to band such men together is not a good idea…what, when they might decide that they are stronger than you? No, for I have dreamed it that you will send someone else—a lone man to perform this task, having first supplied him with an invisible weapon that the moon-child and her pack will find baneful even unto death. Aye, and your man shall unleash a plague upon Bonnie Jean and her ladies, one which they cannot survive!*

"An invisible weapon?" Francesco frowned as he repeated the pit-thing's words, voicing his puzzled query. "But what exactly do you have in mind, Father? What kind of weapon?"

All that I have told you is for you to fathom! the thing in the pit answered, his telepathic voice rising and seething more yet as he began to babble. *Have I not stated that my dreams are incomplete? If I could tell you more I would, but the future is a vast confusion of things that are, things that may be, and—stranger by far—things that* have been! *Ah, you think me mad! I see it in your minds. Well perhaps I am. But what of it? What comes to me in dreams is the source of your power; what I learn of the future is a guide that you can follow. Oh,* ha-ha-haaa! *I am in agony! The stretching and flowing is upon me, and my pain is so great that it is almost a pleasure. But let me…let me show you…*show *you something of what your father has become!*

They knew what their father had become, and moved back from the pit as something rose up its shaft—something that surged like rising dough in an oven, overflowing itself, churning like so much pale red- and purple-veined lava—something with eyes, some of which saw but others that were glazed, blind and insensate in features that formed, collapsed and reformed on a great bloated mushroom of a head and the heaving flesh supporting it!

An extension—it could have been a rubbery, inflated hand—reached up to touch the electrified grill. Only a touch, but knowing, tentative; until hot blue sparks arced and sputtered, and it was at once snatched back!

And with the cavern's glaring lights and electrical systems buzzing and flickering, with the shadows advancing and retreating, dancing on the hewn rock walls and stalactite ceiling, the Francezcis backed off and shielded their minds as best possible against the pit-thing's mental shrieks of pain, rage, and loathing as it sank down once more into its prison.

In a moment more the systems settled down again and the Old Ferenczy's insane and seething thoughts were withdrawn, shrinking into his melting mind. Then as the brothers departed, climbing up through the foundations and cellars of Le Manse Madonie, all that remained of their father above the well's wall was the stench of alien, singed flesh and a drifting waft of foul black smoke that quickly dispersed.

Francesco was silent during the climb, but as they emerged into the upper floors he spoke up. "That old bastard down there deserves his 'tribute' I suppose, but I only wish he didn't put on me so. He has never liked me, not before his change and certainly not now! But his words—what he raved about sending just one man on this mission, and something else he said about bringing down a plague on Bonnie Jean and her lot—that has set my mind to working. *He* may find the future deceptive; he knows the requirement but stops short at understanding the means, but the answer is in his words, I'm sure."

"You're sure?" Anthony repeated him. "Then tell me, what do we do?"

Francesco nodded and looked thoughtfully at his brother. "I think we should first contact our chemist friend in Bulgaria about not one plague but two, or perhaps even three. And, if he can fulfil our needs, then we must find—how shall I put it?—our plague-bearer, a means of delivery. One man, and preferably one that we've found wanting from time to time. Why ruin a good thrall if we can make one last use of a bad one, eh?" And chuckling darkly to himself, for the moment he would say no more…

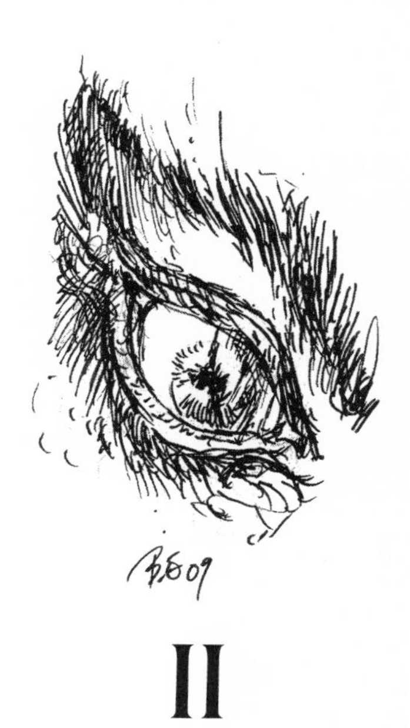

II

Several weeks later, on the white sand beach at Crimdon Dene on England's north-east coast, Harry Keogh caught himself giving more than his usual amount of thought and attention to the monstrous subject of vampires; more specifically, their diversity. Because unlike other men—such as the horror movie-makers, the writers of weird romances, or tellers of tall tales in general; and for the time being leaving aside the large percentage of so called "superstitious" or "unenlightened" or "backward" peoples world-wide who were castigated for such "outrageous beliefs"—the Necroscope knew for a fact that indeed such beings existed. And not just the half- or once-human variety that inhabited the pages of macabre novels or late-night cinema screens.

Oh, Harry had known his fair share of the real thing—much more than his fair share—but recently he'd been given to wonder about the possibly *un*fair attitude of rather more run-of-the-mill men than he himself, not only to the so-called, allegedly fictional undead but also to the actual, factual *Desmodus* and/or *Diphylla;* and, to remain in the realm of the scientifically accepted or acknowledged, not merely to the bats of such loathsome habits but to each and every other of the entire catalogue of blood-sucking species.

Just how or why such a morbid train of thought, the Necroscope's deliberations on the nature of vampires—and this on an otherwise perfect summer's day—just what had set his metaphysical mind working on it: that was a combination of things.

First, the bronze figure of a young man had come dripping from the waves, shaking his head to send salt water flying from his longish hair, with a spent speargun and goggles in one hand and the other's fingers in the crimson gills of a large, white-bellied flatfish. The blood, as red as any man's, dripped from a gash in the fish's head where it had been shot. But it wasn't the blood that had claimed Harry's interest; rather it was when the fisherman took his knife from its sheath to clean the fish, then wrinkled his nose in disgust as he cut away some apparently unclean thing from the fish's still palpitating underside.

And: "Fish-lice!" the man had explained to his bikini-clad girlfriend where she reclined on a blanket, causing her to pull a wry face and lean away from him and his now limp catch. "Parasites!" he'd gone on. "Blood suckers. But they've done little or no damage, and he's a very fine fish. I'll get him filleted in town and we'll fry him up for supper tonight."

And seated close by with his back to the first of the crab-grass-topped dunes where it sloped back from the breeze off the sea, Harry had wondered to himself: *Oh, and what does that make you, or rather us? I mean, who is the bigger monster: the fishlouse for doing the job slowly, but doing it in order to live, or the human being who kills for sport with no real need, then devours the whole fish as a single evening's meal?*

Oh, the fish-louse was the vampire, all right, but what of the man? A common or garden carnivore, Harry supposed, as most Homo sapiens are, though not of necessity. With the fish-louse, however, it was very definitely an entirely instinctive matter of necessity—indeed of survival...

The fish was quite dead now. Its pain was over, and in the near vacuous liquid flux that passed for extinct fish thoughts, it wondered what had happened; but the Necroscope sensed relief rather than the astonishment and growing horror he would expect to find in the deadspeak of more self-aware sentients.

Then with an abrupt shake of his head, as if to clear it of such thoughts—having realized just how morbid his reflections had become—Harry put aside the dead fish's vague abstractions from his mind...only to notice in the next moment a seashell, with the point of its clockwise spiral protruding from the sand at his feet. And without thinking he leaned forward and scooped it up. But even before giving his discovery a closer inspection the Necroscope knew what he would find.

He could feel it all around him, everywhere. Why, the very beach—the sand itself—was composed of dead things; often as not a direct result of vampirism! Perhaps not the dictionary definition of vampirism, but nevertheless a great many if not a majority of the shattered shells of which these sands were made had been the victims of blood or plasma depredation: They'd been *sucked dry* by predators from other mollusc species.

Harry knew it was so; he saw evidence of it in the precise, circular crater or concave bore hole below what would have been the shell's operculum, its tough protective cap.

Of course, the cap was no longer in place; neither it nor the fragile creature it had once protected. Some dog-whelk had drilled its way in to reap a rich reward.

Vampires, *faugh!* If Harry listened—if he concentrated his metaphysical mind on the otherwise inaudible, sub-etherial flux of what passed for thought or cognizance in creatures even less sentient than the bronzed young fellow's dead fish, such as the beach's broken mollusc shells—he could "hear" the faint background hum of myriad…but myriad what? Not minds as such but the soft sighing echoes of lives that were no more. It was just another facet of Harry's deadspeak, his unique ability to communicate with the dead.

As for the *un*dead—well, the ones that he had met up with, and those he had put down, making them more *truly* dead—their cognitive powers in both life and death had been far more sure, more deliberate, and infinitely more deadly. It was ever a cold thing, conversing with the dead; but speaking to expired, once-human vampires, even in that final interminable condition they called the true death…that might easily freeze a man's very heart and soul. But not Harry's…

Not that the Necroscope had done that in a while; at least, he didn't think so. But his memory—perhaps his mind—well, things hadn't seemed to be working right for quite a while now. There was some kind of blockage…but while he couldn't remember why, he wasn't allowed to question or puzzle over that…

And again, *faugh!* For some reason he just couldn't get them out of his mind, his thoughts: vampires! They were quite literally legion. Every creature that flew, walked, crawled or swam, all of them had their own special versions. And men, Homo sapiens as a species, had quite a few. The common louse and all-too-common crab-louse were two of the better known; but what of the pond or marsh leech? Not only a parasite of Man but also almost every other warm-blooded species! As for liver flukes—trematode worms of tropical climes that infest a man's liver until it takes on the aspect of Gorgonzola?—what on earth are horrors like that doing...*on* Earth? By comparison the mosquito seemed harmless!

Suddenly angry with himself—at least attempting to force all such notions to the back of his mind—the Necroscope stood up and dusted himself off. He had never been much of a one for sunning himself. Indeed recently he had found that half an hour at a time was all he required; more and he would burn. But that last was a thought which cancelled his frown and refashioned it into a smile, albeit a wry one. Having had dealings with creatures for which a single stabbing sunbeam meant absolute agony—while a surfeit meant a smoking, crumbling death—Harry would be perfectly content as long as the sun merely irritated him!

Well, so much for putting all such to the back of his mind! Along with that other thing that wouldn't let him be—the real reason he was here, constantly nagging at him—it seemed that vampires, his knowledge and memories of the damned things, just wouldn't go away. They were like so much wormy old furniture in the cluttered rooms of his meta-physical mind: unwanted but apparently permanent fixtures. Not surprising, really; he was what he was, and indeed *who* he was, in large part because of them...

If he hadn't declared war on the first of his vampires, and a Great Vampire at that—Boris Dragosani, Wamphyri!—he would never have come into contact with the brilliant long-dead scientist August Ferdinand Möbius in a Leipzig graveyard. Möbius had first invented or noticed the weird anomalies of his now famous eponymous Möbius Strip: a one-sided surface with only one edge, made by giving a strip of paper a half-twist and joining up the ends. What subjects

Möbius had pursued in his lifetime, however, he'd continued to work on in the afterlife: a general rule with dead people as the Necroscope had long since discovered. But the topology of homeomorphisms had been just one of the scientist's interests, while his specialist subject had been astronomy. And in order to continue studying the planets, stars, and the universe in general, even lying dead in his grave Möbius had found a new use for his knowledge of topology in the strange properties of a mathematical plane of existence which he had named the Möbius Continuum. And he had shown the Necroscope how to use it.

Harry would use it now, but covertly. For he couldn't allow anyone to see him take his departure.

The beach was fairly well crowded, but a promenade over the sea wall sported a small brick building that displayed stylized male and female figures to advertise the usual amenities. Feeling sand moving in his shoes, Harry headed for the toilets. But on the promenade he paused to seat himself on a bench and empty his shoes, then stood up and stared one last time at the beach, taking in the scene from one end of the bay to the other.

A little time passed as the Necroscope's intense gaze roved from one group of holidaymakers to the next; and to an observer, if there had been one, it would have seemed obvious that he was searching for someone. As in a hundred and more other places he had visited, however, that someone or ones—namely his missing wife and infant son—were nowhere to be found. And since they had been his principal reason for returning to this place which he and Brenda had enjoyed so much in their time together, Harry had no reason to prolong his stay.

In the gents' toilet he found an empty booth, entered and turned the metal locking knob. (Let the attendant wonder later how the door had been locked from within, and yet the booth had been left empty—which it would be shortly!) Then, closing his eyes, Harry conjured Möbius math and on the darkness behind his eyelids—like symbols on the monitor screen of a vast computer solving an incredibly complex mathematical problem—he called into being a stream of decimals, fractions, algebraic equations and Arabic cyphers, non-Euclidean and Riemannian configurations, to send them cascading in a dizzily mutating, seemingly endless display from top to bottom of his "vision."

"Seemingly endless," yes; but a moment later, as if frozen in the eye of his mind, he recognized a certain fantastic formula. At which a "door" opened in the darkness where no door had ever before existed, and the Necroscope took a single pace forward and stepped through it—*through* the Möbius door and likewise through that now redundant region of space-time where the door of the booth had been—into the Möbius Continuum.

There beyond the door lay the ultimate darkness, the primal darkness, which existed always, even before the universe began. It was a place of utter, absolute negativity; not even a parallel plane of existence, because nothing *existed* there except in the most unusual circumstances...such as Harry's being there. And Harry knew—he understood—that if there was ever a place where darkness lay upon the face of the deep, this was it. Yes, it might very well be that region from which God had commanded, *Let There Be Light,* causing the physical universe to split off from this metaphysical abstraction. For indeed the Möbius Continuum was "without form, and void."

Any other man would have panicked, would have felt he was falling into nowhere forever; and it might well be forever in a place with no space or time, and so no time in which there was *time* for change! Yet as unique and inaccessible as the Continuum was, still it was Harry's secret place, his refuge. For the Necroscope was scarcely a stranger here, and he most assuredly was *not* any other man.

He knew the co-ordinates he required: Only let him visit a place in the actual, physical, three-dimensioned universe once—thereafter he would always know how to return to a space-time location forever lodged in his mind. The co-ordinates this time were those of a small, coastal hotel room in Scarborough, Yorkshire. He and Brenda had stayed there just once, teenage lovers in an age when fresh young couples had been viewed with suspicion by prudish hotel proprietors. That age—only four or maybe five years past—was gone now, and so was Brenda. But the coordinates remained.

It was a sad, perhaps funny thing, but from pre-teen times to marriage Harry had known Brenda as well as his own image in a mirror. Yet now, when she had been gone less than four years, he sometimes couldn't remember how she'd looked. And looking at her photograph didn't help; more and more it was as if he gazed on the face of a stranger. Of course, it wasn't Harry who she'd deserted but Alec Kyle: the fact that *her* Harry had become someone else, and at least in his looks was a total stranger.

The Necroscope could understood that well enough: as yet he himself wasn't entirely used to being—well, to put it plainly—this completely different person.

Such were his thoughts as he stepped through a Möbius door into his room and without pause went into the bathroom. It was the mirror: Every now and then he would feel this desperate recurrent need to look at himself in a mirror. Not vanity, not by any means; perhaps even the opposite. Harry wasn't even sure he *liked* the man who looked back at him! This fetch, this ghost of a man, however solid, whose body—ten years older than his own would have been—was now his.

Frowning, he studied himself closely. *Himself*, yes, for he must accept that now. His hair was russet-brown, plentiful, and naturally wavy; but in the last three years a lot of the luster had gone, and strands of grey were now visible among the brown. His eyes were honey-brown, too, vastly intelligent and knowing, and (strange beyond words) incredibly innocent! Even now—for all they had seen, all that he'd experienced and learned—they were innocent. For Harry had never asked or intended to be what he had become, or to do the things he had done. But he *had* done them.

His teeth were strong, not quite white, and a little uneven. They were set in a mouth that was unusually sensitive but could also be cruel, caustic. He had a high brow, a straight nose, and cheeks that seemed just a fraction sunken. Not surprising, that last: Kyle had been a little too well-fleshed for the Necroscope's tastes, and he had worked hard to rid himself of the excess weight. This hadn't mattered much to Alec Kyle himself with his height, whose work in E-Branch had more usually been sedentary; but it mattered to Harry. Bad enough carrying those extra years around without all that extra weight! And:

"Damn!" Harry muttered under his breath, and shook his head where he stood staring at himself. And then *to* himself: "Do you know something, chum? I think I'm actually getting used to you!" There was no answer, just a wry grin which gradually faded…

Now then, why was he back here in this room? Mainly because he wasn't quite ready yet to return to Edinburgh. It would have been just as easy to base himself at home; with the Möbius Continuum at his command he could have based himself anywhere! But if he was back in Edinburgh, the

Necroscope knew where he would be spending his time—or his nights, anyway: with Bonnie Jean, if she wasn't too busy with her girls at B.J.'s wine bar in the city. But while she had become the love of his life, and albeit that it was a very odd love affair, still the absence of Brenda—her disappearance—was very upsetting, galling; and still he felt he must track his wife and baby son down if only to ensure that they were okay, fit and well and not suffering any kind of hardship.

As for his feelings for Brenda: Harry knew they were fading now if not already gone entirely. He had found that contrary to the old adage absence—at least in his case—had *not* made the heart grow stronger. Three years and more, much of it spent in fruitless, soul-destroying search, had only served to blunt his affections, especially since he had found B.J. or she had found him.

And that was why he was back in his hotel room: because he had promised to stay in touch, calling B.J. every day. Truth to tell, Bonnie Jean had *told* him to call her every day. She knew what he was about—his ongoing search and all—which apparently made little or no difference to her affections. But B.J. wasn't the sort to admit to jealousy; and anyway, she was aware that Harry's search was a matter of duty, an acceptance of personal responsibility as he saw it. No matter that his wife had fled him, he still must satisfy himself that she and the child were secure, whatever their location and situation.

B.J. never rose until late, rarely went abroad during daylight hours. She revelled in darkness, loved the night and the moon, especially at its full. It was now past midday; she would probably be abed still in her rooms above the wine bar. But the Necroscope knew there was a telephone on her bedside table.

When he dialled her number there was a pause of one or two seconds before a growling, softly Scots accented voice queried, "Aye? It's B.J. here—who's callin' the noo?"

"It's Harry," he told her, already feeling her spell flooding over him. And immediately:

"Ah! Mah wee man!" she said: words that Harry could never resist, carrying a post-hypnotic command unbreakable as carbon steel chains. "Where are ye, Harry?"

"In Scarborough, Yorkshire," he told her. "But I think I'm done here now."

"Good!" she said, at which he believed he detected a degree of relief in her distant, telephone-metallic voice. "So, you'll be coming home soon then?"

Truly amazing, he thought, half-smiling to himself and just a little irreverently, *how B.J.'s Scottish dialect can come and go like that!* An eccentricity or idiosyncrasy…Oh really?

But anyway: "Yes, I'll be back tonight." (As the Necroscope he could be there instantly, of course, but how to explain that to her? He couldn't, so instead he would spend the afternoon at his house near Bonnyrig.) "Should I come to the bar later?"

"Oh, but you'd better!" she answered. "It's been only a few days—what, a week?—since your wanderlust, your search, took you away from me again, but I've missed you." Then that note of concern crept back into her voice. "There's…there's perhaps a problem. Here in Edinburgh, I mean."

"A problem? What, with the wine bar, or your girls? Someone sick, maybe? What sort of problem, B.J.?"

Another pause, until:

"Oh, it'll keep until ye're back, mah wee man. And if ye're back early…maybe we'll have a wee while to oursel's, before openin' hours eh?" B.J.'s voice was less troubled now, even seductive, with her warm Edinburgh accent firmly back in place.

That voice, and those words…oh, B.J. knew how to do it! Harry pictured her in his—in her—favourite position, with her backside raised, her face side-on in a pillow and her sweet mouth open, gasping—or snarling? Tonight, in Edinburgh, yes.

He went downstairs to the desk, checked out, and paid the skinny, weasel-like proprietor in cash for the few nights he'd spent here. He hadn't needed to stay here; he couldn't be sure that he'd ever want to be back this way again, but in any case it wasn't his style to leave a trail of bad debts behind him.

The man counted his money and cocked his head on one side. "And your suitcase?"

"Still packing," said Harry. "One or two items, that's all. It'll take a minute."

The other nodded. "Well, you get home safe, and come see us again some time." *And that's precisely why I've paid you,* Harry thought, going back up to his room.

He had literally a couple of items: spare slacks, socks, an extra shirt, washing and shaving kit. And it didn't even take a minute to throw them into his battered old suitcase. As for the skinny little proprietor: Watching the stairs for a further half hour, he still didn't see the Necroscope leave.

And neither did anyone else…

III

Some fifteen days earlier, about 11:30 p.m. in Sicily:

Mike Milazzo—now a vampire, but once a "made man" who had got above himself in New York and been required to flee home to the Old Country—had been called to attend the brothers Francezci at Le Manse Madonie: not a good omen. Common soldiers were only rarely invited to visit with the Francezcis in their mountain retreat, which normally occurred only when there were questions to be answered; and Mike's activities had never been less than questionable. Moreover, this was his second visit. He considered his past as his car groaned up and around the precipitous route of stone-walled or metal guardrailed hairpins—the only route of access—to the high plateau.

Mike, a darkly handsome, third-generation Sicilian-American thug, had been caught banging his capo's slut wife at her Hamptons home. Still the boss's wife, she was now scarred for life, her mouth slit open so wide she could give blow-jobs to rhinos, and no young Turk (or Italian) was ever likely to find her fuckable again. Only Milazzo's "made man" status had saved him from similar treatment. Oh he'd been badly beaten, but at least they hadn't rearranged or enhanced his features.

And so he'd come back here: back "home" to an uncle also in the Mob, who had reduced him to a soldier in charge of collections and corrections in Palermo. But just like most dicks, when Mike's was hard it had no conscience, no memory, and absolutely no respect for the usual conventions. By all means take advantage of those you prey upon—which is simply the nature of the work, "the business"—but do *not* fuck their virgin daughters! Men can be coerced into paying for your so-called "protection," but only as long as they, *and their families,* are protected.

Mike's uncle had been bombarded, overwhelmed by complaints. Moreover, despite that Mike was paid a decent percentage of the produce of his rounds, he was not above "skimming" the take, to such a degree that his uncle's profits were much reduced. Also, Mike found himself accused of dealing drugs within a neighbouring boss's territory, and his use and abuse of this same capo's young prostitutes had made him more than a mere nuisance; badly beaten high-price girls do not attract high-roller customers.

No more than a year in the Old Country—and no sooner established, albeit shakily—and already Mike Milazzo had become a problem. He had seemed ungovernable, quite beyond the control of his uncle; so that finally the elder Milazzo had asked the advice of the Francezcis, who despite their apparent youth were his "Godfathers" in everything but name.

Their response had been quick in coming—they would "talk" to the wayward young thug—but they had demanded carte-blanche in his handling, in whatever advice or punishment they found it necessary to hand out. Wholly sick of his nephew's often threatening behaviour even towards his superiors—which included the elderly capo himself!—Vito Milazzo had agreed readily enough. Frankly, he didn't give a damn what the Francezcis did to Mike; Mike was already dead where his uncle was concerned. A man offers a helping hand to the undeserving, no account, illegitimate son of a brother long gone the way of all flesh in America, and this jumped-up bastard should immediately take advantage, start muscling in around the territories, crapping all over his benefactor's business and generally fucking him over at every opportunity? No, Mike deserved whatever he had coming—but *not* from his uncle. No way! Forget about it! Family values, and all that shit. But, as Vito's cousins in America would probably have it: "What are you gonna do?"

All of which had occasioned Mike's *first* visit to the Francezci citadel in the Madonie mountains, which was something he would *never* forget; though from the brothers' point of view it might appear that it was already forgotten. Hence this second summons, or so Mike suspected, but only in part correctly.

Now, driving his car up the winding mountain road, fearful and apprehensive in the knowledge of his most recent misdemeanours, as his headlights lit up the luminous arrow warning signs at the hairpin bends, Mike once again remembered in detail that first visit. And vampire that he now was, still he shivered uncontrollably...

Then too the time had been approaching midnight. The Francezcis had this complaint apparently, this photophobia: an aversion to light, especially sunlight. They saw no one and were seen by no one during daylight hours. Chauffeur-driven in their black limo—whose specially tinted windows were opaque to the glances of curious passers-by—their presence might be suspected or even observed by night in Palermo, Bagheria, or some other town more local to their place in the mountains. For there in comparative privacy, in secluded rooms or on the reserved balconies of some of the island's finest restaurants, the brothers would hand out advice, share invaluable intelligence, and discuss business concerns with Sicily's top Mob bosses...but never in daylight.

There were of course excellent reasons why they restricted such outings, meetings, and conversations to the dead of night, one of which the arrogant, overly self-assured, quick-tempered Mike Milazzo—as he had been then—had been about to discover for himself...

In the courtyard of Le Manse Madonie, Mike had been met by two Francezci henchmen who had frisked him rather sloppily. One of them, who stank of too much costly after-shave, had taken his automatic. Then they'd ushered him inside the ancient, mazy old mansion, and left him in a dimly lit, marble-floored room whose walls were decked with rich tapestries and gilt-framed pictures and whose furniture was of mahogany and old but supple leather. The big oval table at which Mike was left seated was of marble, gold-rimmed, with a wonderful mosaic of multi-hued marble chips so arranged as to display a two-metre map of Sicily. As for the tapestries and paintings: When Mike's eyes had grown partly accustomed to the shadowy gloom, he had seen that the former hangings depicted foreign lands—chiefly Romania and the mountains of Transylvania—while the pictures were mainly portraits.

Hung sinistrally, anti-clockwise, to represent the line of descent of the Francezci family (or at least its twin brothers, for it could only be them) there were at least two dozen of the latter dating from ancient times to the comparatively modern:

a thousand or more years of the dynasty's male offspring. And all of them—apart from their dress, their postures, the artistic styles of the various periods, and the natural aging and darkening of the earlier works—all of them looking amazingly similar if not exactly alike.

After a while, angry at his treatment—that he'd been kept waiting like this, with his nerves on edge in the silence, the solitude of this large room—and as his eyes grew more fully accustomed to the dim lighting, Mike had decided he didn't much like the way the faces in the portraits seemed to be staring at him. Rising, he had crossed the floor to take a scowling closer look at them. And that was when the Francezcis had appeared.

From their picture on the wall to their physical presence, Mike saw immediately how right he had been. The twins, pale as they were, seemed paradoxically more darkly handsome than Mike himself; and it had been wholly obvious that they were the men in the most recent of the portraits. Indeed, they might easily have sat for all of the paintings! That last had been a fleeting thought...the young thug could scarcely have imagined it as a matter of fact.

Without pause the brothers had then called him back to the table and waited for him to reseat himself before they commenced what he had imagined would be some sort of threatening interrogation or "interview;" but in any case a "frightener."

And one of the pair had opened with: "Mike Milazzo, as you are known. You know who we are—or if not, you *will* know soon enough. I'm Francesco Francezci and this is my brother Anthony. Your ill-advised activities, far too many of them, have come to our attention for our consideration. However, before we determine what's to be done with you, do you have anything to say for yourself? Any excuses you might care to offer by way of explanation? Any redeeming features you think we should know of?"

Looking from one to the other, Mike had suddenly found himself sneering. Why, these guys couldn't be too many years older than he himself! And: "Godfathers, you?" he'd snorted, relaxing back into his chair. "I should explain myself—offer 'excuses'—to you? Oh really?" *Ha!* Let the old men of the Sicilian Families kow-tow to such as these, but not Mike. Everything he had heard about the brothers—not that he'd heard a lot—what did it all add up to? Nothing much: a bunch of hooey was all! False gods, these guys, and nothing more.

And as the brothers had glanced with raised eyebrows wonderingly, perhaps speculatively at each other, he had continued: "You're like a pair of rich, spoiled snails, too scared to drag your shells into the light; scared that someone is going to see you, know you for what you really are: a pair of fucking frauds, that's what! But Dons, Godfathers? Don't make me laugh! I don't know how you've conned the old Mob guys in Siracusa and Palermo all this time, but you don't con Mike Milazzo. You two? Why you wouldn't last twenty-four hours in America! So *fuck* having this little chat with you guys. Me, I'm out of here!"

Daring, ridiculously bold, but Mike wasn't just muscle. His senses had been honed by a short lifetime of danger in America; he'd been aware of furtive movement behind him, someone or ones moving closer, and he'd smelled again the expensive aftershave of the Francezci soldier who had lifted his gun from its underarm holster. His harangue had been provocative, insulting, and aggressive…but it had also had a purpose: to put those men behind him off guard, give them the wrong impression, make them think he was stupid, all mouth and no brain.

Well, it was true enough: He sometimes mouthed off, got to breaking balls with the wrong people; but he could also back it up. He had the speed, the strength and the know-how, and it was time he showed these Francezcis just exactly who they were dealing with here. His gun may have been taken, but they had missed the slender, razor-edged knife in the sleeve of his lightweight jacket. Redeeming features? Oh, he would show them some redeeming features!

Mike hadn't known when exactly the brothers' men had entered the room, there must be doors other than the one he had come in through. But as a shadow from behind him had darkened almost imperceptibly he had known for sure they were there, known also how to react to their threat. With the smell of aftershave growing stronger, he had slammed back his chair with every ounce of his strength, directly into the knees of both men, and was gladdened to hear at least one bone crack and a sharp yelp of pain. Then, turning as he started to his feet, he'd lashed out at the nearest target with a flat hand whose fingers were stiffened to rock hardness: a slicing blow to the throat.

The man with the popped knee was already down, squirming in agony; the other—the one with the aftershave, who had lifted Mike's gun—had been sent staggering, clutching at his throat where Mike's blow had smashed his Adam's apple. One glance, and Mike had climbed his chair, toppled it, been on the choking man in a second; one hand in his greasy hair while the other patted his jacket, dipped into a pocket and came out clutching his own weapon. And as easily as that he'd rearmed himself.

Then Mike had taken a moment, all of half a second, to aim a kick at the downed man's throat and put him right out of business, rammed his gun in Mr. Aftershave's ear and, still clutching a handful of his hair, maneuvered him down to the floor and kneeled behind him, using him as a shield. He hadn't even required to use his knife and it was all over, or so Mike had reckoned. But he had reckoned without the Francezcis.

They had looked at Mike where his weapon was now pointed at them, and as they rose to their feet their movements were surprisingly smooth, unruffled. They appeared unafraid, even unconcerned! And again Mike had seen them glance at each other speculatively...or perhaps with new-found resolve? And:

"So then," the one called Anthony had slowly nodded, leaning forward to rest his knuckles on the table. "It would appear you are well capable of looking after yourself." And smiling in his way—a smile as cold as the face of the moon—he'd continued, "Given time these men will recover, of course, but still you dealt with them in short order and severely. You have small regard, it seems, for your whereabouts and your...situation." In its way a question, it was delivered with a raised eyebrow.

"These 'men' of yours are useless," Mike had replied. "Boys doing a man's job—which doesn't work. This one smells like a woman, and he didn't even put the safety on my shooter!" Saying which he had returned the muzzle of his automatic to that one's ear. "As for his 'recovery:' if I put a little pressure on this trigger he won't be recovering, believe me! Not with his brains—if he ever had any—all over your nice shiny floor!"

"Believe you? Oh, we *believe* you!" Francesco had answered, almost conversationally. "With his brain ruptured, ripped apart by a bullet, he would be very definitely dead. Which is as good a way as any to kill such as him, certainly."

"In fact," said Mike, rising and releasing his victim, hurling him onto his side on the marble floor, "I'm surprised these guys have any life left in them at all!" He was frankly puzzled that both of the seriously injured soldiers were indeed showing signs of recovery, not squirming so much as trying to sit up!

"Oh?" Anthony had laughed, moving around the table and that much closer to Mike. "Is that so? But you see, my young friend, they have a *great deal of life*—well, of sorts—remaining in them even now. They are very tenacious creatures, Mike, even as you yourself would appear to be. But with them it is…it's a far more recent thing, something in their blood. You might even say they were reborn, recreated with it. While in you it's pure instinct, the natural skill of the predator."

"That's correct," Francesco had agreed, also moving closer. "And you are very fortunate, for it may even be possible we can find a use for such skills…*after all!*" That "after all" had sounded oddly ominous, hinting of a brutal fate barely avoided, but Mike had been given little enough time in which to consider or worry about it.

For while speaking to him—unaccountably and without Mike realizing it, yet startling him and shocking him at the last—the Francezcis had somehow contrived to approach him by moving over the floor in a rapid yet deceptively flowing, indeed effortless fashion. Until now, suddenly, they were at point-blank range!

Mike had fallen back a short pace; he tripped on one of the groping figures on the floor and barely managed to maintain his balance. But despite his sudden confusion—the rising tide of unaccustomed anxiety, uncertainty he felt welling deep inside—he had retained sufficient control to continually shift his aim from one Francezci to the other and back again, taking no chances but covering both of them, despite that it seemed they were unarmed.

And it was during one such split-second shift, with his gun in motion, swinging half-way between the brothers, that Anthony had grown bored with the game and acted to end it. As for Mike: He hadn't even seen the other move—it had happened that fast! But in that single, blurring, unbelievable split-second, Mike's gun hand had been grasped in slender but vise-like fingers, the safety catch on his automatic had somehow been applied, and the weapon itself had been taken from his fist with such force that he'd felt certain his hand must be broken!

What had happened, Mike wondered? Was something wrong with him? Had he suffered a stroke, passed out or something, if only for a second or so? And what had changed—what was *different*—about the Francezcis? Their eyes in the gloom were now...what, feral? Yes! Luminous as a cat's eyes at night, they flared sulphurous yellow in the twins' vilely grinning faces, like small lamps burning on Mike. And the monstrous *looks* of the brothers; their features, changing; the way their lips writhed back from scarlet gums—gums that tore as they sprouted terrible teeth!

Or was it possible that these anomalies were simply hallucinations, delirious illusions, symptoms of whatever was wrong with him? Was he still entirely conscious and not nightmaring? And if so, how was it that the men he had so severely injured, indeed crippled, *were already rising to their feet!?*

By then survival had been uppermost in Mike's mind, and he had fumbled with his jacket's sleeve at the cuff, squeezed it, and tried to close his fist on the ugly blade that sprang into view...only to find that his fingers were still numb, unable to obey him. And his knife had clattered to the marble floor.

And finally Mike had felt himself staggering. Incapable of keeping pace with or even comprehending what was happening to him, he might well have lost consciousness, collapsed from the sheer shock of it—had he not been held effortlessly upright by Anthony on one side and Francesco on the other, their slender but amazingly powerful hands like crutches in his armpits. And when one of the brothers—but which one he couldn't have said—had clapped a handkerchief soaked in some kind of anesthetic over Mike's nose and gasping mouth, he had been utterly incapable of doing anything about it.

So that darkness had swiftly followed…

IV

Following which time had lost all meaning to Mike. He had felt there were periods—moments, at least—when he was awake, but mainly he had slept; he had slept, nightmared, and dreamed scarlet dreams. The brothers Francezci: their rabid, grinning faces dripping blood!...the biting pain that Mike felt whenever one of them, sometimes both of them, were near...the burning pain in his throat, beneath his jawbone, sometimes in his wrist...the drowning sensation, of swirling into oblivion, spiralling away like a spider down a plug hole.

He had been in a box—no, a coffin, in a cavern—a place that was sometimes lit, more often in darkness...and Mike had sensed something nearby that tossed and seethed and lusted. But lusted for what? Perhaps for him? And he'd felt empty and tired...so very tired. So tired indeed that later he would remember thinking: *Is this death? Surely this is how death feels!*

But three days later, when Mike had woken up, he'd finally come to understand his error: that his initial weariness wasn't death but merely the prelude to undeath! At which the brothers had told him how it was going to be from now on…

They had been genuinely impressed, even the Francezci brothers, impressed by Mike's so-called skills, his killer instinct: that he had tackled two of theirs and so damaged them as to incapacitate them however temporarily. A pair of bodyguards, vampires, albeit it "common" vampires, downed by a mere man—an entirely *human* being! And when he had learned what they were, those two, then he had understood what Francesco had meant with his words: "With his brain ruptured, he would be very definitely dead—as good a way as any to kill such as him…"

"Such as him:" an undead creature of the night. In fact two of them, laid low by Mike but by no means permanently. And that was how they had recovered, or begun to recover, so quickly: by reason of a certain "something in their blood," with which they had been "reborn, recreated," by the Francezcis—just as Mike had now been recreated by them.

And as Francesco had explained it to him down there in that deep cavern, after releasing him from the narrow crate where he had lain for three days and nights, "Oh, it has its advantages, Mike, but it also has certain disadvantages, naturally. For example: You are no longer your own man but belong to us; you are 'in thrall'—as the saying goes—to the Francezcis. And for once and for *always*, throughout the rest of your life, you will obey us or suffer the consequences.

"As for the advantages: You were strong, but now you are so much stronger! Your five senses, while they were very acute for a mere man, are now twice as sensitive...which is ample justification for what you said of our two men—our 'boys,' as you had it—who would certainly have had your measure had you been any less self-sufficient, less talented. You took them by surprise, yes, but that is no excuse; needless to say we were *disappointed* with their efforts. It seems they had grown soft in our service, slow and careless, and far too sure of themselves. But then again, they were the least and most recent of our thralls, who you won't be seeing again...at least, not as they were.

"So then: stronger, faster, more aware—with all of your passions doubled and redoubled, which you'll use sparingly, and never indiscriminately—you are now a great deal more than you have ever been. And you will live...oh, a *very* long time! For you are undead, Mike, and will feed on the lives of others. But you must always remember: You can never show the world what you are. You will keep your name, your identity, of course, and you will ever retain the guise of an ordinary man; for anonymity is synonymous with longevity. But only let men see the real you—let them discover you for what you are—and they will hunt you down as others have been hunted before you."

Then Anthony had spoken up. "Mike Milazzo, while you were a 'made man' in America, now we have *re*made you! But just as your American bosses had rules, so we have them in addition to those my brother has spoken of. First of all, you can *never* make more like yourself. The blood is the life, it's true, and for sustenance you may take what you need as you need it, but *never* drain a man—or girl—to the last drop! Kill someone like that and you make a new vampire; but one without understanding, ignorant of the dangers, who may bring retribution to your doorstep. And for the same reason you may *never* use our name nor even mention it! Make no attempt to avoid us, or try to escape our influence by flight; don't even *consider* such treachery. We have familiar creatures superior to the weaklings you dealt with, thralls who will track you down to the ends of the earth and either destroy you or return you here, to us. And Mike, there are other ways—far more painful, lingering ways—to kill such as you than by shattering your brain with a bullet!"

As Anthony paused, then Francesco—grinning at Mike, glaring at him through blazing eyes—had nodded knowingly in agreement with his brother, before adding: "Oh yes! Indeed there are *other* ways! And now you must come with us, for there is someone who may wish to meet you—and something we want *you* to meet."

Still dazed and unsure of his whereabouts, his condition—in fact praying, even a hoodlum like Mike, praying he was still asleep and nightmaring—he could only obey and walk unsteadily between the twins, across the floor of the great cavern towards what seemed to be the wall of a well. But it wasn't a well, and half-way to it Mike had felt once again that sensation of something stirring, seething, lusting: something in the pit. And to his enhanced vampire sensibilities it seemed he could even hear a voice, growing louder and ever more demanding:

For me? Is he for me? A girl would be better, but I am ever hungry and my needs are great. For what you have given me…I am grateful, certainly, but you promised *me a girl!*

Worse still, Francesco had at once *answered* what the terrified hoodlum had hoped or prayed was only his imagination, only a voice in his disordered head:

"Yes, father, and I will deliver, but I need a little time. As always, there are difficulties to be overcome. However, this one is not for you. He is one of ours, a new one who displays a degree of promise, but who yet needs convincing of the requirement for the strict rules that regulate our organization—and more especially of the penalties for disobedience."

Oh, indeed? had come an answering grunt, sounding more than a little disappointed. *Is it so? One of ours, freshly made?* But a moment later: *So be it. Perhaps I can 'rise' to the occasion, eh? Oh, ha-ha-ha!*

The voice had "echoed" like a belching blast from an alien abyss, and finally Mike had known the truth: that while it was indeed in his mind, it was not of his making; that it had been *put* there by some fearful Other! And though he had tried to dig his heels into the rough floor of the cavern, still the Francezcis had dragged him to the pit, where its electrified grill had been raised up on its gear, leaving a gap of just eight or nine inches.

And as the three had arrived at the rim of the pit, so its grotesque occupant had come surging up the shaft, and Mike had known the true meaning of horror! He might have struggled free but the Francezcis had held him as easily as they might hold a child, letting him gaze with eyes that only half believed what they were seeing—until the pallidly pulsing mass of the *thing* in the pit had ejected through the gap between the wall and the grill an assortment of clattering bones, flensed to a gleaming whiteness.

At which Mike's already slack jaw had dropped more yet. For among that pile of debris he had seen a pair of polished, human skulls, *and he'd known at once, instinctively, who they and the rest of the bones had belonged to!*

"Just one of many penalties of failure," Francesco had told him then. But Mike could never be entirely sure that he'd heard him correctly. For at that point his stunned mind had been shutting itself down, while his shuddering body was already totally uncooperative; so that without the brothers to keep it upright, it would have crumpled like an empty sack to the cavern's dusty floor...

Thus Mike Milazzo had become an agent in thrall to the Francezcis, one of their local watchers—a spy not only on those Old Men of Sicily he'd once called capos but on the world in general—an errand-boy, runner, and talebearer; and, but only very occasionally, to ensure that he kept his edge and remained practiced in thuggery, a brutal enforcer when the brothers had need of such. And for a while—a matter of weeks, almost a month—Mike had stayed within their guidelines, obeying their rules to the letter.

But a leopard may not change its spots, and being just such an animal—not merely a predator but a carnivore and a drinker of blood at that—he'd soon found the restrictions placed upon him frustrating, even demeaning. He had new, superior muscle to flex, and yet was on a leash; with teeth sharp as knives, still he was muzzled by masters he never saw, who contacted him where and when they wished and other than that were less than shadows to him. Why, for all Mike knew he might never see the Francezci brothers again! He would be in their service, always, but never more in their presence...at least he could always hope not!

And finally he had surrendered to his nature: his "pure instinct," as Anthony had had it...but in fact an instinct that was anything but pure. And the guidelines and rules had at once flown right out the window.

As a result of which:

Here Mike was in his car where he'd brought it to a momentary halt, staring across the stony, barren roof of the plateau, at the low, dark, sinister silhouette of Le Manse Madonie where lamps glowed a dull yellow above the gate in the high perimeter wall. Here he was in answer to his second "invitation," in fact a command, which he dare not refuse; and as before there was no excuse for the things he had done.

And remembering all too clearly what those things were: how he'd let enhanced passions rule and used them indiscriminately, and how he had used a name he should never use, Mike shuddered. He shook like a leaf in a gale however briefly, uncontrollably, and waited until the tremors ceased before slipping his car into gear and starting it rolling along the narrow, weedy, badly weathered track to Le Manse Madonie…

This time Mike didn't have so long to wait; or rather, the brothers were waiting for him! And there was little or no preamble when all three of them got seated at the same table in the same room as last time. But once more there were others in the room: Francezci thralls who, for the moment, remained in the shadows. Mike was fully aware of them, however, detecting their presence with heightened vampire senses. He hadn't seen them—not even with night-penetrating eyes, for just like him they were expert at hiding in the gloom—but he could smell them and hear their breathing, and every slightest rustle of their clothing.

As to their purpose there, these bodyguard vampires—especially now that Mike knew the brothers' nature, their strength and near-invincibility—that was a nagging concern that raised his apprehension to almost insufferable heights. Perhaps it was simply that the twins didn't want to dirty their tapering, long-fingered hands on such as him. But in any case that was all the time Mike was given to wonder and worry about it, for no sooner was he seated than Anthony was rebuking him with undeniable accusations:

"Mike Milazzo, it seems there's only one thing I can say in your favour—you didn't run when we asked to see you! But then again, if you had so much as *attempted* flight you wouldn't have made it to the airport or the harbour, would never have boarded a plane or a boat. No, but you *did* think about it, didn't you?"

Mike nodded, found his voice, and said, "Yes—until I felt their eyes on me, imagined myself in the cross hairs and sensed their fingers on the triggers. And I figured: This way I'm dead meat. Then I figured: No, I'll be *un*dead meat! Whoever they are they won't kill me but take me up into the Madonie—which will mean I've made my last mistake!" Mike paused to moisten his dry lips and throat, and in a sudden, desperate burst of speech continued: "Now listen to me...I mean please, *please* listen! The last time—the first time—I was here, you asked if I had any excuses for the things I had done, mistakes I'd made. And no, I admit I didn't. But this time I—"

"Be quiet!" The other twin, Francesco now snarled, his eyes burning like coals in a face white with rage. "Who asked you to speak? And for that matter—who permitted you *to speak of us!* Weren't you in fact *forbidden* to speak of us? So what happened, Mr. Milazzo? Is your arrogance such that you think you can defy the Francezcis? And as for that girl you drained—weren't you warned about that? Well of course you were! Fortunately you are not the only agent in our employ, supposedly 'in thrall' to us. No, for we task our most trusted agents with watching the watchers! One of them was watching you: She was covering your tracks and got rid of what you made. Fortunate, too, that the girl you vampirized was a whore, and whores occasionally vanish. The sea around Sicily is deep...though not deep enough, apparently."

As Francesco paused so Anthony took it up again. "Mike, are you asking—do you really *dare* to ask—that we listen to your so-called excuses, your lies? Your *lies,* yes! Because there can be no genuine excuses, not for your blatant disobedience to our explicit instructions, our rules! So now *you* listen, and listen very carefully. For far below Le Manse Madonie there's a cavern with a deep, dark well—a pit, actually. And in that pit—"

"I know! I know!" Mike gasped, cutting the other off before he could complete the threat. "You showed me what's in the pit. But please don't...don't...*just don't!* And I really can explain what...what happened, what went wrong. And you're right: There is no excuse. But there *was* a reason, if you'll only hear me out."

The brothers looked at each other, appeared to relax a very little. And after a long silence Francesco nodded and said, "Go on then. Tell us about it. Give us your 'reason.'"

Mike breathed deep, moistened his lips a second time, tried hard to keep his often uncouth manner of expression, his thuggish tactlessness in order; this despite feeling his fear beginning to turn to frustrated anger. And *that*—his volatile temper—was one of Mike's major failings, where he'd fallen short far too often before, and where *once* had been too often for the Francezcis! So that right here and now would be the worst possible place and time to lose control yet again, for all that his heightened vampire emotions were coming to the boil inside him.

For which reason he calmed himself as best he could, licked his lips once more, and finally found some words which he could only hope were the right ones. "You...made me," he said. "You took what I was—*knowing* what I was—and made me more, much more. I was twice as strong, I lusted twice as hard, and when I was angry I raged! But suddenly my lust was a murderous thing. Oh, I had had plenty of girls before, but I'd never fucked and sucked one to death! Now, being the way you made me, I could do that—and I did! Yes, she was a whore, and she'd known plenty of men before me, but never one *like* me. I believe she enjoyed it! Even as she faded away, died, she was...she was smiling!

"But at first—before the girl, and before I was used to being what I am—the blood of others had made me sick. So I'd tried to eat my favourite foods as usual, good Sicilian foods. But they made me even sicker, and I let myself get hungry. *Too* hungry! And then...*then* there was the girl."

"Yes," said Anthony, "and now you can stop, because we know the rest of it. She was a capo's girl—one of Mario Stefano's—and you had had her before. *And* you'd been warned off! Indeed she was one of the reasons we called you up here the first time around, because we didn't want any trouble brewing between Vito Milazzo and his people and the Stefano family. And yet you went back to her and—"

"—*And* she was one great fuck!" Even knowing he was losing it, perhaps because he was losing it, Mike couldn't contain himself a moment longer. "So before I even realized what I was doing, I'd done it to her! But it was you guys who did it to me!"

"And now you are accusing us!" Francesco snarled, coming to his feet, scowling again, and leaning over the great table.

"I'm not accusing you," Mike answered, sensing movement behind him, and feeling them approaching out of the shadows. "I'm just stating a fact. And as for the rest of it—"

"Haven't I told you we *know* the rest of it?" Anthony snarled. "They found her floating off Castellammare bay.

Stefano's people knew who to blame; they'd seen you with her, remembered you from those previous troubles, the sit-down with your uncle. But this time there would be no sit-down. They came looking for you—luckily for them in daylight, for they were merely human—and found you sleeping at your place in Palermo. Naked, with three guns at your head and a hot afternoon sun blazing outside, you couldn't run and certainly couldn't *out*run a burst of bullets from their Uzis! So before they could cut your balls off or splatter your brains or both, you told them you were one of our so-called 'made men' in Palermo! You *dared* to invoke the Francezci name! And in fact the only secret you kept to yourself was what we'd 'made' you into! If they had discovered *that*...right now you'd be screaming your life out in a certain pit!"

Francesco took it up. "Knowing our reputation—our name if not our nature, and fearing it—too cowed to do anything else, they let you go, gave you your miserable life. But should we do the same? Perhaps not. For you've not only broken the rules and failed us, *Mr.* Milazzo, but caused us a great deal of embarrassment and trouble in the bargain!"

There was movement behind Mike and he sensed it, knew there were Francezci thralls, if not how many, approaching out of the shadows. He felt his body tensing, coiling inside like a spring but there was nothing he could do about it. Without his weapons and with Wamphyri twins just waiting for him to make a move, he had lost his edge and knew it wouldn't be like the last time.

But what the hell? Whatever was coming he couldn't just sit still and wait for it! And so he came surging to his feet.

In that selfsame moment: "Hey, Mike," said a sinister voice from close behind. "I've got a little something for you."

Self-preservation—Mike's instinct, pure or otherwise—at once surfaced. Whirling, he saw in the forefront a thin, feral-eyed man with three other, vaguer figures behind him. He failed to recognize any of them, but was instantly aware of the gun in the thin man's hand. Without pause he sprang headlong, toppling his chair...and in a sort of mental slow-motion, as if frozen there in midair, he saw the muzzle of the gun give a jerk where it was pointing at him.

The thin man almost blurred as he moved aside, and Mike hit the floor. He made a single attempt to rise but found it futile...with an anaesthetic dart pinning the collar of his shirt to his neck he simply couldn't get up! Even enhanced vampire blood was powerless against a drug that worked *that* fast!

Then as a whirling darkness descended, smothering his mumbled, incoherent protests and dragging him effortlessly down, he was dimly aware of Anthony's shadow falling on him, and an echoing, rapidly receding voice that faded away completely almost before it had time to advise him: "Calm yourself, Mike. You'll wake up soon enough, undead but alive, for we have work for you yet. And it's a job for which you seem eminently suited..."

V

It was surely one of the strangest of liaisons, one of the most peculiar and even mismatched affairs of the heart. And to Harry Keogh and Bonnie Jean Mirlu alike it had become one of the most puzzling yet simultaneously satisfying adventures.

It had been that way almost from their first meeting—more properly a collision—one night in London, where they had both been hunting the same psychotic killer. On that occasion Bonnie Jean had probably saved Harry's life, and in return the Necroscope had saved B.J. from a whole lot of trouble; though if they had known who or what they were saving events might easily have proceeded in the opposite direction.

As it was Harry had found her magnetically attractive right from the start and sexually irresistible ever since. It was the animal in her, he thought, without fully appreciating the irony of his appraisal. But it was a fact that Bonnie Jean was a sexy woman and "a real Looker," as the Necroscope had once heard her described. Tall, slim and slinky—but entirely natural with it—she seemed ageless; she could be anything from twenty-two to thirty-five. As for her roots: possibly Eurasian? She could be, from the shape of her eyes. As oval as almonds, and almost unnoticeably tilted, they were a deep hazel flecked with gold; and when she was angry Harry might even think of them—and of B.J. herself—as feral! And her hair, bouncing on her pale shoulders, seeming black as jet but grey in its sheen, especially at dusk. And those legs of hers that went up forever, or not quite forever, but certainly to that place where Harry's entire world invariably dissolved into some soul-sweetening essence whenever they made love.

The rest and greater part of her—which from the Necroscope's point of view included B.J.'s personality, for he wasn't utterly besotted; it wasn't simply Bonnie Jean's body he lusted after—was equally, undeniably attractive. Her ears, large but not obtrusive, flat to her head and elflike, with their pointed tips often as not hidden in the bounce of her shining hair; her nose, tip-tilted but hardly "cute;" her mouth, perhaps a fraction too ample, yet still delicious in the curve of its bow. And last but not least her teeth: Harry couldn't recall ever having seen teeth so perfect or so white.

"What sharp teeth you have, Bonnie Jean!" some inner voice, perhaps his own, would sometimes begin to advise him. And: *"All the better to—"* it would continue, until another voice, B.J.'s voice, or his memory of it, would cut in with:

"Ah, no! Don't go there, mah wee man. For that's no a verra safe place...no safe at all."

That was part of how she controlled him, while at the same time giving herself to him, without understanding the fascination that she in turn felt in Harry's presence. For what was he after all but a mere man? If that's all he was. Or was it possible he was something more? And looking at him—just thinking of him, the way he looked—she would wonder about that: about the facts in the former life of her mystery man, this stranger who had become her lover.

While Harry's frame was solid enough he was far from muscular. He wasn't handsome, or only moderately so, and in fact his features—apart from an occasionally bitter expression and the wry curl of a caustic upper lip—were generally unexceptional; but not entirely. The anomaly lay in Harry's eyes: those honey-brown eyes that were so obviously, vastly intelligent and knowing while yet, paradoxically, seeming so incredibly innocent.

Or was Harry's apparent innocence also some kind of facade, a cover to conceal what lay beneath? As for his past: B.J. had questioned him about that; about some of it, anyway. Indeed, he hadn't really needed to be questioned. Only start him off about his lost wife and child and he would tell it all, or almost all. But there was always something in there that he kept back, kept to himself despite the spell of obedience—those post-hypnotic commands—which she had lodged in the deepest recesses of his subconscious or semiconscious mind.

Harry had mentioned in passing certain powerful friends in London: members of a secret security organization with which he had once been connected. But while B.J. had tried to dig deeper he would mention it only in passing, and immediately change the subject. Obviously his loyalty came uppermost; some deep-seated sense of moral integrity—some vow he'd made which he couldn't revoke or renege upon—caused Harry always to avoid or obscure the issue, denying B.J. access. While this was frustrating, however, still she admired his mental tenacity and high principles. It wasn't just anyone who could hide even his innermost secrets from such as Bonnie Jean Mirlu! If her "wee man" could be faithful to some old vow, pact, sentiment, or agency from years gone by, how then to a girl, woman, moon-child who he took to his or her bed each night?

Thus she was reassured, for there could be little doubt but that his love, not to mention his lust—or for that matter her own—were very real. And indeed B.J. sensed that Harry's feelings for her might well last for ever; certainly for as long as he himself lasted. As for her fondness for him, if that was all it was...well, that was a different matter entirely. For B.J. had certain loyalties of her own which hadn't weakened down all the decades. Or perhaps they had. For knowing that the time was coming when she must, or should, let Harry go—and where, and to whom he would be going—knowing these things disturbed her greatly. And despite that she had known men before and that her Master in his high place knew and accepted it, this time Bonnie Jean felt guilty...

These were her thoughts as she looked at Harry where just a moment ago his eyelashes had flickered and his breathing quickened. Downstairs B.J.'s girls worked the wine bar, and here she lay naked with her lover, wondering at his most unusual nature. And oh, what an irony in that! When her own nature was anything but usual! A low purr, or more properly a growl, escaped Bonnie Jean's throat as she went to kiss his neck...but only a kiss, never a bite. No, for his blood might be as sweet as Harry himself, and that would never do. She wasn't sure she'd be able to resist it!

Harry's eyelashes fluttered again, and with a mumbled, "Uh? What?" he rolled onto his side, more surely facing her. And now she got down from the bed, to begin dressing herself as quickly and quietly as possible. He had been sleeping for a little less than two hours since they'd made love; but B.J. had experienced his apparently boundless energy before, and she didn't want him to wake up and see her naked. Not just now, anyway.

She felt hot, flustered; she had work to do downstairs, her girls to supervise, her guilty wayward thoughts to pull together into some semblance of order! And she knew she could do none of these things with his eyes and then his hands upon her.

Huh! But wasn't *she* supposed to be the great beguiler!

Harry yawned, stretched, propped himself on one elbow, and said, "Uh! B.J.? Where are you going?"

"Where there's work for a body," she answered. "Downstairs, mah wee man. It's late, aye, but there's two hours yet till the midnight hour, and I like tae do mah share. Ye can stay here if ye so desire, or come down and have a wee dram. The one thing I ask ye tae remember: There'll be the usual bunch o' likely lads in the bar, and ye mustn't let it be seen that we're—"

"—Lovers?" Harry finished it for her, and continued: "because they all of them like to think they stand a chance, eh?"

"Somethin' like that, aye," she nodded. "But they don't."

"I'll get dressed and come on down," he said, swinging his legs over the edge of the bed. "But I'll skip the wee dram. I'd prefer a glass of that wine of yours, that's if you keep any in the bar?"

B.J. smiled and nodded an affirmative. Oh, there was a full bottle of her wine in the bar, all right—kept out of sight of the customers but within easy reach. One glass of that and he'd be ready for bed again—this time to sleep. Then, after closing the bar, she'd be able to talk to her girls, her moon-child pack in private, reminding them of the dangers out there in the streets and the night and warning them against...against what she couldn't say, not yet. But something, she felt sure. It was in the night air; and, in addition to what two of her girls had told her, B.J. could sense it.

As if her thoughts had been spoken out loud, Harry appeared to answer them, saying: "Bonnie Jean, I came back early because you told me there might be a problem here in Edinburgh—but we haven't talked about it. Do you want to take five minutes, tell me what's troubling you, what's going on?"

Halfway to her bedroom door she considered it for a moment, and thought, *Well, why not?* For Harry's mind would be too dull, blunted, after drinking her wine. Tomorrow, in the light of day, he might not remember what she'd told him; her words might have flown right over his head without making sense to him. That was something of the nature of her wine.

B.J.'s wine: a potentially addictive soporific, and on certain occasions an aid to her hypnotic powers:

Its recipe had been old when most of Earth's sciences were yet unborn, and even alchemy was in its youth. B.J. didn't know what the ingredients were, but she knew something of their origins, where to find them today, and how to brew them up and make the brew potent. Certain of the herbs, pollens, and resins came from the Greek islands—also from Bulgaria and further afield—and in the long ago some had come from the Far East with the Hsiung-nu in the form of precious balms and medicines. But that was centuries before men learned how to synthesize such chemicals. The wine had been known in Manchuria and Sinkiang, also to the Takla Makan Desert's Worm Wizard cultists, and later to the Arab alchemists of olden Irem, the City of Pillars. In the 14th century it had been used by the Bulgars—who were good chemists and vintners both—and by the Serbians and Ottoman Turks, to ward off the Black Death, which also had its source in eastern parts.

After that its secrets had been lost to mankind in the reel and roil and turmoil of a troubled world. Lost to mankind, perhaps, but not to B.J.'s Master—who remembered all such things from the olden times—and not to Bonnie Jean herself, in whom, over the years, the dog-Lord had invested many items of esoteric and otherwise forgotten knowledge…

"Well?" said Harry, getting dressed. "Is there a problem or isn't there? Someone being a nuisance in the bar, maybe—like that Big Jimmy bloke: that jealous clown who fancied you, found he couldn't have you, and decided to take it out on me? Well at least he tried, and we can do without more like him! I mean, he was a roughneck, a street fighter, and dangerous! Hardly one of your 'usual bunch of likely lads,' now was he?"

"No," B.J. replied, "and neither are you! He was twice your weight, built like a gorilla, and you handled him like a baby!" And Harry made a mental note that her Edinburgh accent had completely disappeared again.

"It was him or me," he answered, and shrugged. "I suppose I was lucky." But he knew that luck had nothing to do with it. It was simply that he'd called on a dead friend—an ex-Army PTI, a Physical Training Instructor and expert in a handful of martial arts—to come to his aid and lend him the know-how to deal with the jealous bully. Of course Bonnie Jean didn't know about that; she only knew what she'd seen. And:

"No, you weren't lucky," she shook her head. "You're *good*, Harry, and you know it! Anyway, I was glad to see Big Jimmy get his…though I can't say the same for the bar's furniture!"

Harry frowned. "You know, I'd have bet good money that he'd be back for more, that one. That he'd be out looking for me one dark night. But we never have seen him again."

Ah no, not quite true! she thought, sitting down beside him on the edge of the bed as he buttoned his shirt. *The reason* you *haven't seen him again, Harry Keogh, is because me and my girls sucked that big bastard dry one night when you were away!* While out loud she said, "Oh, I shouldn't worry about him. I did hear that Big Jimmy has moved out of the city to Dunbar or somewhere down the coast. And a good thing he *didn't* come back, or by now there'd be no furniture left in the bar at all!"

Harry leaned towards her but B.J. pulled away, saying, "Now hold! You asked me a question—about that problem I mentioned—and I'll tell you about it, if you'll only be still! Just lie there and listen...*mah wee man!*" But that last was spoken with a certain irresistible emphasis, and in a moment the Necroscope was as pliable as putty where she pushed on his shoulders until she'd stretched him out again with his head on the pillows. And then:

"Very well," B.J. said, her voice low, husky, but in no way seductive. "Now *listen!*" She reached out a hand and turned down the bedside lamp, and in the dull golden glow her eyes were yet more tilted, almost triangular, animal-like and totally undeniable.

"Harry, it's the middle of the moon's cycle," she began her narrative, outlining post-hypnotic orders or instructions which would lie submerged or "forgotten" in the Necroscope's subconscious mind, but ready to resurface the moment he needed them. "A *waning* moon, Harry," B.J. continued, "which won't be full again for sixteen days. So why is that important, eh? Well, while I'm hardly what you would call a weak woman, still I am at my weakest beneath a waning moon. Now, normally I wouldn't involve you but deal with this thing myself; except this time I'm of a mind that the threat is *other* than normal—indeed, *far* from normal—and I can feel it drawing closer, even looming over us.

"You see, this isn't a Big Jimmy sort of threat, Harry. Indeed, I would rather a dozen Big Jimmies than this, whatever it is! And that's the problem, for I just don't know—but I know what it *might* be.

"I want you to remember certain of the things I've told you before. Not on the surface of your mind but deep down inside it. In the days to come *remember,* and be aware of the danger; for I fear it's a danger not only to my girls but also and especially to me and my Master in the heights up North. But because we are together, you and I—and even though you're not of the pack—who or whatever this threat proves to be may believe it necessary first to deal with you in order to get to me and mine. Now, is all of this understood? Answer me."

Harry lifted his head an inch from the pillows, nodded, and fell back again. And with his unblinking gaze fixed on hers, he said, "You think someone or thing is coming for you and I might get in its way, putting myself in danger."

"That's right!" she replied. "But if I am correct in what I more than suspect, it won't come in the form of a human agency. This is a dark thing, Harry, from dark times. Now let me remind you:

"My Master has powerful enemies in the world. They hate him because he is unlike them; his *nature* is not like theirs. While I am less than he is—and my girls less than me—still they hate us also. They know that without me, a moon-child, sworn to serve Him in the Mount, he would be weakened, easy prey to them and their agents. And now I'm given to suspect that one or more such agents could be here in Edinburgh.

"As to what makes me think so:

"In the last few days, no more than a week, two of my girls have been followed by a furtive figure, both times on their way to late-night duties in the bar. On the first occasion the male figure kept its distance, head down and collar up, following in the darker shadows of the street's buildings. It quickly turned away as Zahanine, my black girl, looked back as she reached the door to the bar; turned away and vanished into an alley. But he was so quiet—a wraith, like a shadow in himself—and there was something else about him: such an evil emanation that Zahanine felt this dreadful premonition. And it was such a terrible foreboding that as she entered the bar I saw how she shuddered! I am sure you'll appreciate, Harry, that my moon-children, like myself, don't take fright any too easily, and that when they do there is usually a very good—or very bad—reason!

"That was the first time, and despite that it might simply be an attack of nerves on Zahanine's part—for she is known to be a little skittish on occasion—it sounded the alarm. But to tell the truth and because we were aware of Zahanine's periodic panic attacks we weren't too much concerned, just a little more alert and cautious. Which is as well, for the next incident was much more ominous.

"It was the youngest of my girls, Kate, who lives less than a mile away and always walks fearlessly to the bar on even the darkest night. And why not? For night is her element, as it is mine. But while Kate's habitual route is the shortest, it passes through a maze of some of the city's oldest, bleakest alleyways. Just three nights ago she walked that same route, and for the last two or three hundred yards of cobbled alleys was aware of soft footfalls from somewhere behind her—but ever closing the gap!

"Are you listening, Harry?" She stared hard at him, at his unchanging features and almost glassy eyes. "Can you understand what I'm telling you?"

Again the Necroscope lifted his head, nodded and said, "Yes, I understand. She was being pursued—possibly."

"Huh!" B.J. snorted. "Not just 'possibly', mah wee man, but definitely! Now let me get on:

"Kate came out of the alleys onto the street only a handful of doorways from the bar. Glancing back, she saw that her pursuer was very close now: a man all in black, his description was the same as the one given by Zahanine. Ah, but Kate is a feisty one for all that she's young! And so she stood waiting beside a recessed doorway. For if this was just some man—some perverse but otherwise *ordinary* man, who fancied his chances for a quick grope or perhaps something more than that—then she would know how to deal with him. When a man's penis is hard, there's nothing compares with a kick between his legs to soften it up a bit And never forget, young Kate's a moon-child with a moon-child's strength. She had none of Zahanine's nervousness and could take care of herself against most men, be sure. But as for *this* man:

"For all that the night was warm he wore a long black coat, buttoned to the neck, with its collar turned up. And as he came level with Kate on the empty street he grabbed her, forcing her back into the deeper shadows of the recessed doorway. Surprised by his ferocity and speed, still Kate fought back and momentarily drove him into the open. At which, further enraged, he took her by the throat; and now his grip and strength were such that she knew he was no ordinary man! But a madman? Well, possibly.

"She looked to the sky, intending to draw strength from her mistress moon, but all there was was a pale yellow crescent. In her panic she clawed at her attacker—and thought she saw how his eyes lit like dull lamps! What's more, he seemed to be trying to bite her! That is how it appeared to her: that this... this *animal* was intent on fastening his teeth in her neck!

"Ah, but in order to do that he must first release his grip on Kate's throat, where he held her with only her toes touching the pavement. When he did that her feet found purchase, and she was at last able to deliver that kick. It was a blow that would have felled most ordinary men; it should have sent him groaning to the ground. But he merely grunted and reached for her again.

"At that moment a car's headlight beams flooded the street. It was a police vehicle: They patrol this area, however infrequently. Kate's attacker was startled. Releasing her, he uttered a low curse and ran across the street into a narrow alley where the police car couldn't follow.

"The vehicle stopped, and an officer got out to ask Kate if she was all right, was everything okay, and who was the man who had run off? She lied, said her attacker had demanded cash, and she was a little shaken but otherwise all was well. She pointed to the bar's hanging sign, said she was on her way to work, and that she'd be safe here. But no, she had never seen the prowler before, and it had all happened so fast that she couldn't describe him. Well at least that last was more or less true, but as for the rest: how to describe the entire experience? What could she say without having to answer more questions?

"Do you understand, Harry?" Again B.J. paused. "Kate didn't want to attract too much attention to herself, not to mention to me and the other girls! Now tell me—do you know what her attacker was or might have been? Answer me."

The Necroscope's reply came almost at once: "He might have been a vampire," he said, as if that was the most natural thing in the world. While deep within him some facet of his subconscious mind recalled the beach and his nagging, almost obsessive preoccupation with vampires—their many species, from Nature's myriad parasitic creatures to those half-human fiends with whom he'd already had far too many dealings. So then, had that been some kind of precognition? Possibly a side-effect remnant of the brain-dead—now entirely dead—Alec Kyle's oneiromancy? The last vestige of his talent, like an echo lingering on in an empty conch, still extant in the whorls of a brain which now housed Harry's metaphysical mind? Had it perhaps been an inkling of something to come…or rather, of a *thing* that was now here?

It was only an idea, a vague and momentary thought from the innermost recesses of Harry's mind, which was quickly occluded as Bonnie Jean confirmed what he had said:

"Yes! A vampire! An agent of my Master's enemies, it has to be! I believe this morning's newspapers have confirmed it. Some poor woman—a prostitute, or her remains at least—were found late last night in the blazing ruins of her gutted place in the red-light district. She had been beheaded and an accelerant had been used to burn her to a crisp! Now, what do you say to that? Answer me."

And sounding completely detached, disinterested, the Necroscope said, "Little wonder you sounded so anxious when I called you."

B.J. frowned and her mouth fell partly open. She had expected, demanded some kind of answer, but not quite this one. Oh, he was deep, this Harry Keogh! Even hypnotized, still his mind retained something of its integrity, a fact which she had noted on several previous occasions.

"Yes I was anxious," she nodded. "For my girls, myself, and for you. Oh, I know how well you can look after yourself—*mah wee man*—" (that again, with its special emphasis; but in dealing with a mind like his it was surely prudent to reinforce her hold over him from time to time.) And having done so she continued: "Yes, I know that you are fast and strong and clever; sometimes I think *too* clever!" And again she frowned. "But I didn't want you coming here all unprepared, only to run into something like that. That's a measure of how much I care for you…"

And suddenly aware of the truth in those words, and finding herself sidetracked, she couldn't help wondering out loud: "But how much do you care for me? Answer me, Harry."

"As much and more than I ever cared for anyone," the Necroscope immediately replied. "That's how much I care for you."

Now B.J. smiled. "Oh, and what of your Brenda? Answer me."

"I used to love her...I think," he answered. And still he retained his totally relaxed, hypnotized expression, showing no feelings whatsoever. "But Brenda has been gone a long time, and I can't find her."

"And does that pain you?" B.J. found herself fascinated now. "I mean, how are you affected? You may continue to answer me."

"No, it no longer hurts me," Harry answered. "But it frustrates me—because I don't know where they are, Brenda and the little fellow, or even if they're safe and well."

"And you love no one else, just me?" B.J. felt herself softening. This serious business she'd commenced didn't seem nearly so serious now. Oh, it was—yes of course it was!—but so was her relationship with Harry.

"No one else," he replied. "Just you...now."

"Oh?" And as quickly as that B.J. was frowning again. "Just me...*now?* Was there some other woman beside Brenda, then?"

"Before Brenda, yes—and since Brenda."

B.J. was suddenly hot and flushed; she felt her concentration slipping. "You've never mentioned this before! Who else was it, or is it, that you love or loved? Who is she?"

"My mother," Harry replied. "My Ma. She's dead, you know."

And feeling foolish, Bonnie Jean sighed her relief, letting it wash right over her before telling him: "Yes, I know. You've told me before. And you remember her, and love her still, after all this time?"

"Of course...because she loves me."

Ah, the faith of the man! thought Bonnie Jean. *He dreams of his Ma in heaven, looking down on him and loving him still!* For of course she couldn't know the truth of it, and Harry couldn't enlighten her; he had told her as much as he could tell anyone.

Then, finally, it was time to finish this.

"Harry, mah wee man," she said. "I want you to remember all I've told you about this threat to me and mine, and to yourself. Not on the surface of your mind but deep inside it. Will you do that for me?" It was more a demand, a command, than a question.

And the Necroscope responded: "Yes, I'll remember, but deep inside."

B.J. felt satisfied at last. She smiled...then pursed her lips, nodded, and added one last thing. "Harry, I expect you to watch out for me and mine, but not so much that you'll put yourself in harm's way. Is all understood?"

For long moments he was silent; and then unusually, indeed uniquely in B.J.'s experience, a frown had crept onto his brow! It seemed that even hypnotized he could be puzzled, concerned.

And: "How am I to watch out for you, *and* stay out of harm's way?" he queried. "What if I come face to face with a vampire?"

Ah! Now B.J. understood the problem. Her fault, for she had issued what appeared to be contradictory instructions; at least to Harry's way of thinking. And now she corrected herself. "No, Harry! I only meant that you should look after yourself *as best possible.* Is that understood?"

And as the frown disappeared from the Necroscope's face, so he answered, "Yes."

"Well then," B.J. said, sitting back from him. "Now you may get up on your elbow—blink your eyes and yawn—stretch your limbs and come more properly awake. And you may want to give me a kiss before I go down to the bar. You might also want to tidy up a little before you come down. You may begin to do all those things now, Harry."

Harry began to do exactly as ordered, of course; but before B.J. could go down to the bar her telephone rang, and she commenced a long angry argument, in fact a harangue, against one of her suppliers who was trying to apologise for the late delivery of various wines and spirits.

And so it was Harry who was first downstairs...

After sitting at the bar with a small beer, reading the evening paper and talking to one of the girls—conversing in fact with young Kate—Harry was on his way out into the Edinburgh night when finally B.J. came downstairs. She asked what he was doing, and without preamble he told her he thought he'd go out for an hour or so, take a walk in the warm night air.

Immediately alarmed, she leaned close and whispered: "Ye'll do what? Take a walk in streets so poorly lit?" And shaking her head, "That's no a good idea, Harry!"

He raised an eyebrow and for a moment looked surprised; and trying not to frown, B.J. wondered, *Is he just putting it on or what?* But just a moment later he answered, "If I remember correctly, B.J., they were also poorly lit in London that time. Are things any different now? I don't think so."

Controlling the urge to remind him how she'd saved his life that time, she said: "Ye're a contrary man, Harry! Did I no see ye drinkin' that wee beer after tellin' me ye fancied a glass of mah wine? What, has the thirst gone off ye then?

And even if it has, still ye'll be better off here in the bar. For there's all sorts o' weird folk out in the streets this time o' nicht!"

The Necroscope grinned and thought: *Ah, that false Scottish brogue of hers!* Which he knew was mainly for the benefit of the handful of local lads in the bar. And the reason B.J. whispered was because she didn't want those self-same customers wondering at her concern for this "bleddy sassenach," this Englishman who always seemed to be hanging around the bar these days.

But anyway, it was nice to know she worried about him. And:

"Hey, I'm a big boy now, Bonnie Jean," he told her. "Surely you know that? But anyway, I promise I won't talk to strangers, okay?"

Since he was already headed for the exit it seemed it would have to be okay, and B.J. made no further protest. But after he had gone she took Kate aside to ask her what they had been talking about.

"Oh, just the local layout," Kate answered in all innocence, "About mah wee flat, and the route I take tae get here; no that I'll be walkin' it again! No, from now on I'll be takin' a taxi here and back! But he says he likes tae walk the streets—more fool him!" And then, remembering B.J.'s attachment, "Er—but a *verra* nice yin for a' that! I told him he should call in at the garage doon the street, or maybe a stationery store tae pick up a map o' the area. That should satisfy his curiosity, should it no?"

To which B.J. nodded, saying, "Aye, I should think so." But in her heart she suspected that Harry's "curiosity" wouldn't be satisfied quite so easily.

Which was just as well, she supposed—as long as he remembered to look after himself "as best possible." For

B.J. had to admit that so far, and with that one exception in London, Harry had been pretty good not only at looking after himself but just about everything else! Pretty damn good, for a mere man…

…Aye.

VI

It was 10:30, and night's cloak had long since settled on Edinburgh's ancient streets and historic buildings. The last faint flush of a departed sun loaned low western hills a fast-fading afterglow, and likewise silhouetted the famous outlines of the city's towering Castle-on-the-Rock against the deepening black velvet of a sky full of stars.

It was night and the vampire Mike Milazzo's time. And only when he rose from his bed in the grubby room where he had languished through all the hours of day in fear and loathing of the yellow curse, the monster whose seething rays on the building's outer walls—indeed the very *knowledge* of those rays, of their *proximity,* with only eleven inches of fragile brickwork to ward them off—had caused his flesh to creep; and only when he had crossed to the room's small window, half-shuttered his eyes and cringed as he cautiously lifted a corner of dank and mouldering curtain to glimpse beyond the fly-specked pane only the dark of night and sense something of its balming coolness...only *then* could Mike feel truly secure and breathe more easily—

—At least until dawn, when the sun would rise again...

It had not always been this way. In more familiar Sicilian surroundings after those Francezci bastards had taken his blood and turned him, and when the change had taken hold, he'd had at least a little time to get accustomed to the dangers of his condition. But since visiting Bulgaria on the orders of the brothers, and having met "The Chemist," who was one of their agents, those dangers had not only multiplied but were much more imminent. And even after a week and a half Edinburgh was new to him and strange, while the work he had been tasked to perform was not without its own hazards.

Getting dressed by the window and continuing to look out on the night, Mike scowled and cursed the fates—but in the main, and for all that they had appointed him their thrall, he cursed the Francezcis. And Mike's thoughts were poisonous as he remembered the events leading up to this: his punishment, his reason for being here. Mere thoughts, however, could never be as lethally poisonous as Le Manse Madonie's vampire brothers—nor for that matter as monstrous as the man they had sent him to see in Bulgaria...

Mike remembered how he had struggled awake in the confines of a cellar under Le Manse Madonie; how he'd surfaced from a drugged stupor to find himself hanging in chains against a damp, nitre-streaked stone wall. And despite that in those first moments of returning awareness he ached in every fibre of his being, still Mike's first dull reaction before his situation fully dawned on him had been one of relief—that he was still alive!

Moments later, as his painful stirring caused his chains to clank, a Francezci servant had appeared, nodded his acknowledgement of Mike's awakening, and moved silently off again into the shadows. Following which, within just a few minutes, the Francezcis had come to visit.

Barely conscious, Mike's thoughts had been confused, whirling. His only emotion: that soothing sensation of relief for his continued existence, however precarious that might yet prove to be. So that when at last Anthony had spoken to him, it almost seemed to Mike that the "youthful," centuried vampire had read his mind:

"Oh, what's this? Do I see fear, terror in your eyes, Mike? Now why is that, I wonder? Did I not tell you that we have work for you, a job for which you seem eminently suited? But perhaps I was mistaken. Perhaps you're not the man we took you for, not suited at all! For to find you here, so very weak, strung up in your chains…and afraid?"

At which Francesco had taken it up. "And so you should be afraid, *Mr.* Milazzo! How many warnings did you expect? Knowing who we are, and what we are—and what we guard, succour, and *feed* down there in its pit at the roots of Le Manse Madonie—and for all that you are or should be one of ours, a Francezci thrall, *still* your behaviour has been intolerable!"

Anthony had moved closer, narrowing his smouldering yellow eyes and cocking his head a little to one side where he stared as if in fascination at Mike dangling from his chains. Finally he had nodded. "Yes, my brother is quite right: utterly intolerable behaviour! And here in this very house of ours at that! You attempted a *second* attack on several of our very best men! Either incredibly brave, or unutterably stupid! For unlike you we learn from our mistakes."

And at last Mike had found his voice, which sounded from a parched throat and emerged as a strangled croak: "I thought…thought I was a dead man. And it seemed…seemed to me I had no choice but to fight. So I fought, or tried to."

"Yes, which gave *us* no choice!" Francesco had then growled. "Except to knock you out. But in fact we *did* have a choice: We could have killed you outright and thrown you into the pit…or *not* killed you but thrown you in there anyway! Which in the end would be the same but even more… unpleasant. Thank your lucky stars that you're not down there even now!"

At which, once again, Anthony had taken over from his twin. "You see, Mike, we've decided to give you one more chance—one *last* chance—which is why you're chained instead of suffering the worst true death that any undead man could possibly imagine. So then, you're still alive, at least for now, but nevertheless shackled. Why? Because you are too quick off the mark and there may still be a little fight left in you. And if you continue to give us trouble…but no, for we have taken measures to ensure that can't happen." From a pocket in his long black coat he had then produced a hypodermic syringe, tapped it twice with a sharp fingernail, and squeezed the plunger to eject a few droplets of glistening fluid.

And: "No," Anthony had continued, stabbing the needle into Mike's arm through the expensive materials of his soiled jacket and sweat-stained shirt, "we can't afford to have you fight us, for then we'd be *obliged* to kill you and be done with it! Which would ruin our plans for you. Wherefore, this:" And he had held up the hypodermic again, to let Mike see that it was empty now. "You scarcely felt it at all, did you? A mere bee sting, right? From which you feel no ill effect whatever. Not yet, anyway…"

Then it had been Francesco's turn. And his voice had gurgled like thick oil draining from a sump—gurgled with perverse pleasure—when he asked, "Do you recognize the word 'bubonic,' Mr. Milazzo? And, in relation to that needle, can you guess the word's significance? Oh yes! Indeed you can! I see by your suddenly bulging eyes and twitching lips that you know *exactly* what I'm telling you! But are you also aware that the bubonic plague is yet another way, one of the cruellest ways, for the likes of us, or rather, on this occasion the likes of you, to suffer the true death? What, you didn't know that? *Well now you do!*"

At which Anthony, not to be denied some measure of the sadistic pleasure enjoyed by his twin, had explained that Mike had less than a fortnight to seek an antidote in Bulgaria; to visit their agent there, a man known only as "The Chemist," who would supply him with the cure and certain instructions, before sending him off to complete his assignment in Edinburgh, Scotland.

"But of course," Anthony had added as if on an afterthought, "if you should foolishly decide not to follow our orders or The Chemist's instructions, then you'll surely die—in agony! And if you should think to attempt any more ridiculous heroics here at Le Manse Madonie…there's always the pit. But for now, if all I've said is understood, I shall unchain you. Then when you are feeling a little better, my brother and I will explain something of the task you'll perform for us in Edinburgh.

"So then, is all clearly understood?"

After Mike had nodded his aching head, and croaked a single word: "Yes," in reply, Anthony had unlocked his shackles, letting him crumple to the floor. And in a little while, as some of the stiffness went out of Mike's joints, a pair of the brothers' vampire thralls had come to help him move to a more comfortable room in Le Manse Madonie's upper quarters, leaving him there to consider all that he'd been told and wait for the Francezcis to supply him with the rest of their instructions, his orders.

But with what he had supposed was a deadly poison, a veritable plague coursing in his veins, each minute Mike waited had felt like an hour…

Mike had been given "less than a fortnight," perhaps twelve or thirteen days, to visit The Chemist in Bulgaria, obtain an antidote for his alleged condition, receive final orders and certain items of latent equipment, and then journey on to Scotland and the task in hand. Less than a fortnight, yes; but once the brothers had supplied him with The Chemist's address, he'd been there inside twenty-four hours!

Now in this shabby, cheap hotel room in Scotland's capital, as night settled more surely on the ancient city's streets, his thoughts were bitter as bile as he recalled to mind his time in The Chemist's lonely Bulgarian villa in a densely forested area some miles from Gabrovo in the Balkans…

Mike had flown to Sofia, hired a car and driven one hundred and twenty miles to Kazanlak and on through the Shipka Pass to Gabrovo. From Gabrovo a large-scale local map of the region's frequently trackless mountain forests had seen him to the gates of a stone-walled private estate located in a valley between spurs radiating from the craggy spine of the Balkan Mountains: all of this travelling done by night—the night following his ordeal at Le Manse Madonie—so that it was almost dawn by the time of Mike's arrival at his destination.

From a distance the iron gates had appeared rusted, in part ivy-grown. But as a security camera situated in one of the high wall's buttresses detected Mike's approaching vehicle, and after he had halted the car, stepping out into a swirling ground mist and a probing light beam from a verandah under the jutting roof of the gloomy house at the end of the drive, then the gates had been activated, causing them to swing open on well-oiled hinges. For of course Mike had been expected.

Having parked on a gravel-strewn hard-standing close to the house—a chalet-like wooden structure half hidden in the shade of close-towering, guardian evergreens—a place that seemed in excellent order, despite age-darkened timbers and the mistiness rising from some nearby stream—Mike had climbed the steps of an oak-boarded stoop to a heavy front door, also of oak. Now he understood why the house appeared in such good order: It seemed to have been constructed of quality oak from the ground up.

The door had an old-fashioned iron knocker in the shape of a clenched fist; but even as Mike had reached out his own flesh-and-blood hand to the hinged hand, so the door had swung almost silently open, revealing The Chemist where he stood smiling his welcome.

In that frozen moment of time Mike would have found it difficult to say what precisely he had expected; but it would never have been the bent figure at the threshold, or the warming glow of a fire behind him, reflected from a hearth deeper within the house. And after that moment had passed:

"Come in, Mr. Milazzo," the figure had stepped to one side, gesturing and inviting entry. "Please come in—and welcome to my house—my young visitor from Sicily! Come in man, and make yourself at home. For if you're not comfortable then neither am I, and I *insist* on being at ease in my own home!"

The Chemist's voice—for all its robust-sounding message—had been no more than a whisper, fragile as last year's wizened leaves. And as if to corroborate an impression of great age, he leaned on a walking-stick and shuffled as he led the way down a corridor to the main or living-room.

As Mike had followed close behind his small, frail-seeming host, so the apprehension, the nervous tension he'd experienced throughout his journey dissipated. For The Chemist, who or whatever else he might be, was scarcely someone to be afraid of. Or so it seemed...but perhaps Mike should have remembered how he had felt much the same way about the Francezcis at one time...

"A hearth-fire, on a warm summer night," he'd observed, as he seated himself where his shrivelled host indicated, beside a small occasional table.

Taking a chair directly opposite him, The Chemist answered, "I prefer the glow of a fire to electrical light. My eyes, much like yours, are not suited to bright lights, and especially the light of the sun. Also, the atmosphere—the air in this wooded valley—is damp for much of the year. It comes from the stream that runs to the rear of the house, where a waterwheel supplies the power for my basement laboratory. As for the fire, it keeps the rest of the house dry."

While he talked in this direct, open manner, Mike had studied his host more closely. The old man was bald, wrinkled like a walnut, heavily veined in what Mike could see of his scrawny arms, and wattled with folds of loose skin under a blunt chin. If what he had said about the light, more especially sunlight, meant what Mike suspected it meant, then the current state of The Chemist's health didn't say much for the alleged longevity of vampires!

He had soon discovered his error, however, when he bluntly inquired: "So you're like me, in thrall to the Francezci brothers, eh? A vampire, and one of their agents!"

His host had meanwhile risen and shuffled over to a drinks cabinet. As he returned with glasses and a bottle, Mike's question brought him up short. Frowning, and apparently surprised, he barked: "Eh? What's that?" But then as he flopped back down into his chair: "Ah! I understand! Yes, of course! But no, I'm not like you or the Francezcis. No, not at all. With me it's a disease of the eyes. A photophobia and incurable. Here, have a drink. Then we can talk about why you're here. And don't worry, Mike, for I'm aware that time is of the essence. Meanwhile, try some of *this* essence! Oh hah, hah!" And pouring liberal amounts from the bottle, he had offered a glass to his guest.

Lifting his glass in the glow of the fire, and rotating his hand to cause the dark red wine to swirl, Mike had stared at it through narrowed, openly suspicious eyes. While food—ordinary food—no longer appealed to him, he had at least retained something of his appetite for good wine. The question, however, remained: How "good" was *this* wine?

As if in answer to that question, his host had reached over to clink glasses with Mike, and with obvious relish had drained his own glass and refilled it. Seeing which, Mike had sipped at his wine and tasted its warm, fortified excellence. Then, somewhat easier in his mind, he'd sat back in his chair and allowed himself to relax more yet...

"So," The Chemist had smiled a yellow-toothed smile across the table, "you took me for a vampire! That tells me something: that you are new to your transition. Given time, if that should be your lot, you'll recognize your own kind more accurately and instinctively—the way a dog sniffs out another dog."

"What?" Mike had leaned forward. "If it's to be my lot? But isn't that why I'm here, to earn myself more time? And are you insulting me, comparing me to a dog?"

"Not at all, not at all!" The other had held up his arms in protest, anxious to deny it. "It's just my way of speaking! But I agree: It was a poor and thoughtless illustration of vampire, er, *sensibilities*. And of course you are here to earn yourself more time—indeed, an entire lifetime! Please forgive me."

Scowling, Mike had nodded. "Okay, you can forget about it this time—but in future you better watch what you say and how you say it!" Reaching for the bottle he had refilled his glass, thrown half of it back and felt its warm smoothness going down. Then, after grunting his approval, he had continued: "Now maybe we can get down to business. For it's like you said: Time—*my* time, if not yours—is of the essence."

"Oh, indeed!" The Chemist had answered him with a sharp nod of his own. "But don't worry so, Mike. For while a remedy is at once to hand, it serves no purpose to be in such a hurry. Let's face it, it's almost dawn—and can you travel by light of day? No, I think not. Best that you spend tomorrow here, eh? And be on your way again come fall of night."

That had made sense, for by then Mike had been quite tired; and anyway, the wine was making his head swirl. "Yes, I suppose so," he had answered at last...and been surprised to discover that he slurred his words a little. Also, almost without realizing that he had done so, Mike saw that he'd emptied his glass again. And not only that, but...*but what was this?*

The Chemist was chuckling deep in his throat!

"Why...why are you laughing?" Mike had tried to reach for the bottle, only managing to knock it over. Then he'd tried for his gun in its underarm holster, but his hands weren't working!

"What? Why am I laughing?" His host's gurgling chuckles had fallen silent at once. "I'm just pleased that you've enjoyed my wine so much, that's all."

That's all? Mike hadn't thought so. "Tell me," he had tried not to slur his words. "If the Francezci brothers place so much faith in you—if they think so highly of your skills that they employ you at a distance like this—how come they haven't made you one of their thralls? Or perhaps they have! Perhaps you are…are in fact…in fact a thrall! A fucking vampire thrall! Which would mean that you were simply lying to me like…like this lying…*this lying fucking wine of yours!"*

"Lying, my wine? Well, maybe." The Chemist had replied as a sinister smile spread across his face. "But me? No, never! I am just a man, Mike; but old, wise, and expert in the special arts pertaining to medicaments, balms and lotions, vaccines and antibiotics, and all and every manner of chemical agent, both natural and synthetic; including opiates, toxins, poisons and their antidotes. And likewise almost every physical *disease* that ever afflicted modern man…such as several that will soon afflict you! Yes, my friend, for I have developed the most terrible infections and their cures both; certain of which, er, *sicknesses* you must suffer for a while as a penance for previous errors—also as an incentive to obedience, of course—for which you'll only receive the cures when your work for the brothers is done. Hopefully in time to save you from a very terrible demise…"

There The Chemist had paused to catch his breath before continuing. "As to why the Francezcis never vampirized me: that is because unlike you I am loyal to them who pay me so well, trustworthy in my fashion, and beyond measure valuable to them. More than that however, I suspect that they *daren't* turn me! Knowing what I am capable of as a mere man, can you imagine how I would prosper as a vampire, even as a Great Vampire? Why, given sufficient time and the brothers might well end up in thrall to me! Oh, hah, hah!"

His sick laughter—surely that of a madman—had died away almost immediately, and he'd continued. "As it happens, I'm not interested in being a loathsome creature of the night; for as I have told you, Mike, I have problems enough already with strong light..." And finally he'd shrugged. *"Hmm!* So then, what do you say to all that? That is, if you are still able to say anything at all."

And: "You lousy...lousy old *bastard!"* Mike had managed to mumble, trying to will his limbs into motion and failing; while the room and his senses—enhanced or not—began to spin, turning faster and faster, until finally they whirled him down into darkness...

VII

Almost at once, within no more than two or three minutes as his skewed senses were able or willing to judge it, Mike had recovered just enough that he was able to feel his numb body bumping down cold stone steps, dragged indifferently along by spare but powerful hands at his ankles, into a subterranean room.

The place had been illumined by a soft, clinical-blue light which filtered through his three-quarters shuttered eyelids and caused him to vaguely, dazedly picture himself in The Chemist's basement laboratory. Accepting this, still Mike's drugged brain made little or nothing of it. He had felt no fear but a surreal sense of wonder and a vacuous, dreamlike lack of control.

In fact Mike had no control whatever as he was strapped to a table, felt a blanket thrown over him, and sensed the subdued lighting fading as the power was reduced. Following which he had been left alone in a faint blue gloom which, however paradoxically, had seemed far less malign than the previous darkness and even restful; so that Mike's vampire tenacity—his obstinacy—had at last succumbed, letting him fall into a deep and almost natural sleep…

But if what went before had been dreamlike, the rest was nightmarish. Mike had started awake with streaming eyes, his vampire senses assailed by smelling salts five times as potent as any a person might purchase from a legitimate drugstore; beyond doubt a concoction of The Chemist.

As vivid memories returned and the tears dried on his face, Mike's initial instincts in the blue light of the basement room had been to scramble to his feet, examine his circumstances…then seek out and deal with his tormentor, and harshly! But no, he was still strapped down; and struggling against whatever was binding him only caused burning pains in his wrists, ankles and neck. Then, as his eyes cleared, his captor's withered face had swum into view, gazing down on him. And:

"Ah, I see you're awake!" The Chemist had nodded his satisfaction. "Yes, awake and strong, and your fingers itching to be at my throat, eh? But no, however badly you may want to, you'll do me no harm, Mike; and you will soon come to understand why I had to quieten you down. For if you'd known what was coming…oh, out the window then with all the brothers' rules, instructions and orders—and probably with a poor old Chemist, too!"

While The Chemist was talking, Mike had managed to tilt his head forward enough to see the thin, blue-gleaming metal chains that restrained and apparently burned his wrists and feet. Moreover, he could feel another chain searing his neck.

It was very odd, or maybe not. Normally he would expect to be able to break such chains quite easily, but—

—But once again it had been as if The Chemist had read his mind.

"Silver, Mike," that one had informed him. "It has a chemical composition that is a poisonous acid to such as you. So you can stop fighting it and relax, while I shall endeavour to make you more comfortable." With which he'd turned a wheel, rotating the table into a near vertical position. Then for several long, painful moments the silver chains had burned Mike more yet, but as his feet had touched the floor and taken his weight the pain had slowly died away. Until at last he'd found his voice, which had come scratchily from a throat as dry as sawdust:

"What's this all about, Chemist? Where's the antidote I was promised? Why am I tied up in these silver chains? *And what the fuck is going on here!?"*

The Chemist was a small man; his wrinkled, blue-tinged face had looked up at Mike, thin lips moist and quivering, eyes full of a monstrous fervour, as he replied, "I'll answer your questions one at a time. First: This is all about your *not* doing me any harm. You'll see what I mean shortly. Next: There is no antidote to the *sweet water* with which you were injected! That was simply a ploy, a threat to bring you here, where I shall inject you with the actual thing...*or things!* And the answer to your third question is the same as for your first. As for your last: the answer is this!" With which he had shown his victim a hypodermic syringe, spraying a thin fountain of its blue-glistening contents into the air.

Mike had seen all this before; indeed, it was as if everything that was happening to him was like a recurrent nightmare. And as he had tried to shrink into himself, away from the shining needle, so he had groaned: "You lousy bastards!

You and the fucking brothers—all of you—*bastards!* But listen, Chemist: Don't go thinking you can poison me and then just turn me loose. Best that you kill me outright, now. Because if you don't, then no matter how this turns out you can be sure I'll be looking to kill you!"

But: "No, you won't," The Chemist had shook his head as he plunged the needle into Mike's neck. "And now I'll tell you why not. The brothers had need of a plague-bearer, and you are it." While speaking he emptied the syringe into Mike. "But the bubonic?" he had then continued, withdrawing the needle. "Just that one plague? No, not at all. You see, there are several diseases which are deadly to vampires and moon-children alike. The bubonic is one, and leprosy is another. Also, rabies is a slow but merciless killer, though more especially to dog-Lords and their moon-children thralls. So now tell me, Mike: Can you guess what sort of monstrous mixture is circulating in your blood? Oh yes, you can! I see it written in your wide, wild eyes! And you are right: You are infected with a combination of all three taints, whose poisons are working their way into and through your system even as I speak!"

At which Mike had laid back his head, groaned his frustration out loud, and said: "Then you'd better kill me now, Chemist…for there's no way you can ever turn me loose."

"You're not thinking, Mike!" The other had at once snapped. "You must ask yourself the purpose of all this, which is simply to make you obey and follow the Francezci brothers' orders. For if you don't you *will* surely die! Ah, and now I see that you're listening!"

Mike had nodded, however uncertainly, and replied, "Are you telling me there really is an antidote for all this shit you've pumped into me?" For by then he could see that there would have to be, if he was to go on to Scotland on behalf of the Francezcis.

"Yes," The Chemist had answered. "Yes, of course there is—but not until you've finished your task in Edinburgh. Now then, see what I have here." And he'd moved out of view, returning in a moment to hold up three phials of variously coloured liquids.

And again Mike had nodded. "I see: three supposed cures for three alleged diseases. Three colours, too: red, black and pale yellow. But are the cures genuine, or just another lie?"

"Oh, they're genuine!" The Chemist had answered. "The Francezcis may enjoy their little jokes, but I am The Chemist, and I pride myself in my work. These deadly strains I've developed, they are the real thing, yes, and likewise their cures."

"So what's to stop me from taking them?" Mike had inquired. "I mean, as soon as you turn me loose."

The Chemist had grinned like a madman. "Three small phials: red, black, and yellow, yes...but only two of them are cures, Mike, while the third is an accelerant! Drink the two cures and your diseases will be cancelled, wiped out within the hour. But if you should drink the accelerant—*then you'll rot!* And even more rapidly! So then, dare you choose? I think not."

At which, shaking his head in confusion, frustration, Mike had scowled and commenced to ask, "But then, how will I—?"

"How will you know which ones to consume?" The Chemist had cut him off. "Mike, the Francezcis have agents out and about in the world, including Scotland. You'll be watched, observed most closely. You may not even see your observer, for I know him and he's a veritable shadow among shadows! But he will see you, and he will also be watching your target. He'll know when your task has been completed, and then *he* will supply you with the solution to your problem: which two of my phials you may drink from, and which one to avoid, er, like the plague? Oh, hah, hah!"

"How will the watcher know these things?" Mike had asked.

"Because by then he will have contacted me," The other had replied, "and I shall have told him. That is, *if* I am alive and well. But if for any reason I am unwell or even unhappy—if I should feel indisposed, disinclined—well, you're not stupid, Mike. I'm sure you follow my meaning...?" And:

"Oh, I do," Mike had answered. "So now you can loosen these chains and set me free."

"Ah, no, I think not," The Chemist had replied. "You have a certain look about you, Mike; I'm quite sure you're the impulsive sort and I wouldn't want to tempt you. So I'll just lie you down again under your blanket and give you a shot, and when you wake up at dusk the chains will be gone—as will I. But don't worry, for I'll leave these phials close by. My only advice: Do look after them, won't you?"

With which he had returned the table to its horizontal position, given Mike a shot and left him prone beneath his blanket again. And as the basement's clinical blue light faded Mike had turned his head a little and watched The Chemist climb the concrete steps, seeing no sign of any infirmity about the man, and no walking-stick aiding his quick and agile movements...

The Chemist had been as good as his word and better—or maybe worse. Mike had awakened as dusk was settling; he had found the dimmer knob, brightened the lighting in the basement, and collected the three phials from a workbench, where he found them in a small padded box like a cigarette case. Along with the phials there had also been this note:

Mike—

Behind the curtain in the corner you'll find a caged animal. Just three days ago I used it to test the efficacy of my new synthetic bacilli—you'll know the ones I mean. Of course, as a man you are much bulkier than the poor dog by perhaps six or seven times; also, your vampire blood will try to fight off the infections...and fail. But this is an example of what you can expect should *you* fail. I calculate you have somewhere in the region of eleven, possibly twelve days, before you need to take the antidote, by which time you should certainly have begun to resemble the canine in its cage...

TC

In the specified corner of the spacious subterranean room, while the smell had been offensive Mike had nevertheless opened the curtains and revealed The Chemist's "experiment." He'd felt little or no pity as he at once noted that the dog in the small cage was close to death and quite beyond help; indeed his emotions had been entirely self-centred as he also noted the bursting pustules all over the animal's scrawny body, the madness of hydrophobia, rabies, in its glaring eyes and foaming jowls, and the way its extremities appeared to be disintegrating. Leprosy, surely? Having found his gun with The Chemist's phials and note, Mike might easily have put the creature out of its misery there and then; but no, that would have been the waste of a bullet.

Then, as he had left that poisonous dwelling in the misted shade of the mountains, the thought had occurred to him to burn it down, raze it to the ground; at least until he recalled what The Chemist had warned of the dangers of his being made "unwell or unhappy, disinclined or indisposed"—and then he'd at once reconsidered all such incendiary notions.

Following which, biting the inside of his cheek until blood spurted, he'd driven furiously from the house up into the mountains, and begun retracing his route to the airport in Sofia...

Mike had been fortunate to board a plane to Munich that night. The flight had taken off late; it had lasted for two hours; he had spent the rest of the night and following day in a transit hotel room not far from the German airport. Later, his evening flight to Edinburgh had seen him into the city around midnight, which had suited Mike perfectly. Plenty of time to get himself a room in this seedy so-called hotel, not too distant from his target's wine bar, and then to step out in the night in search of food. Blood, of course.

Prostitutes had been Mike's main prey ever since the Francezcis turned him, and like every big city Edinburgh had always had its fair share of ladies of the night. Now, with Mike Milazzo, the city was also possessed of a *creature* of the night, if not the first of his kind. For indeed the Francezcis had their agent or watcher there, and there was also B.J. Mirlu and her pack. But while Mike wasn't the first, he was nevertheless an especially brutal member of his species.

Within an hour of leaving his room he had found a girl in a maze of steep alleys not far from the great Castle-on-the-Rock. She had taken him back to her place—a pair of grubby rooms in a once-proud building, now a block of flatlets—where they had sex. Following which she'd demanded payment, which Mike had delivered in the form of a bite; indeed far more than a bite, for yet again his hunger and appetite had driven him to the edge.

It was only at the last possible moment, when she was about to fall unconscious or worse, that Mike had recognized her symptoms and remembered the Francezci brothers' precept with regard to making more of their kind. And so, remaining by her side, he had let her sleep, watching over her until he was satisfied she would survive his feeding. Then, in searching her squalid flat, he had come across evidence of the girl's drug addiction, which as an ex-dealer he had at once recognized. He had then reasoned that this was why she'd seemed so weak, which meant that if she died later it wouldn't be down to him entirely. He knew that if he'd drained her to the dregs she would be dead already! And so he had seen no need to cover his tracks: a serious error, as he would discover soon enough. For Mike wasn't "merely" a vampire, he was also a plague-bearer!

The incident had taught him a lesson, however: that he must be more careful in how he conducted himself. If the Francezcis' agent knew he was here and was already watching him, he did not want any sort of adverse report finding its way back to Sicily! For he desired that his life, or his undeath—his very existence—should continue long after this unfortunate episode was over and done with.

And so for eight of the last nine nights he had managed to control his hunger—barely—and aware that time was narrowing down had concentrated on studying the comings and goings of the Mirlu woman and the girls who worked at her wine bar. There had been many occasions when he'd followed one or another of the latter from the bar to their places of domicile and back again, learning the routes which they habitually used, and in the main he had succeeded in avoiding attracting their attention. On one such occasion, however, as Mike had followed the black girl, he had come a little too close and it was possible she had noticed him: the way she'd spun on her heel at the entrance to the wine bar, spun in that abrupt, startled manner, and looked back. But Mike had ducked quickly out of sight and it seemed that nothing had come of it...

Also, there had been that incident four nights ago, when he had thought to put an early end to the game. With the phials in their container in an inner pocket—a pocket which in his paranoia he kept patting to ensure they were *still* there—and with the first small purple lump swelling in his left armpit, he had felt disinclined to bide his time. Why should he, when it would take just one bite, a mere nip, to pass his poisons on to whichever victim he chose to infect?

A single nip, yes! Then, letting his saliva do the work for him, he would "take fright," run away, and in all innocence his victim—believing him to be a sexual deviant or common mugger—would eventually infect the rest of the pack. Even B.J. Mirlu herself...

Bonnie Jean. Ah! It would have been something to single her out for the pathogenetic transfer! But no, B.J. was seldom seen outside her wine bar; and anyway it probably wasn't such a good idea to even consider an attack on the leader of the pack: somebody the Francezci twins had described as "a bitch on the brink of ascendancy."

And so Mike had decided on one of the girls: the young one. She would be the vessel for the dispersal of his poisons. First hydrophobia: rabies, making her sick and feverish, inducing her to do some biting of her own. Then the bubonic plague, or Black Death: one of the worst scourges in mankind's long history. And last but not least leprosy: the so-called "bane of vampires"—or perhaps on this occasion, and more fittingly, "*wolf's* bane?" Or even "werewolf's bane?"

Mike found that last a wryly amusing notion, if not one he could laugh at himself. For all three of these monstrous synthetic afflictions—the creations of a madman, and all the worse for that—were even now making themselves manifest in him. And rapidly!

Even now, yes. And still looking out on the darkening city, he uttered a frustrated, self-pitying, introspective grunt. The purple lumps in his armpits and groin were opening and starting to weep; when he flushed the toilet he could no longer bear the sound, the sight, or even the thought of running water; and more ominous yet, there was little or no feeling in the two smallest fingers of his left hand, which were now grey and stick-like...

And it was that, mainly: the living (or dying?) undeniable evidence that indeed The Chemist's diseases were already burgeoning within him, which had prompted Mike's initial attempt at the contamination of Bonnie Jean Mirlu and her pack by means of a strictly limited attack on the youngest of her girls. And but for the girl's fighting spirit, Mike's rotten luck, and a trick of fate he would have had her. He had in fact *had* her, had been about to sink his teeth in her neck when that police patrol car had appeared out of nowhere!

And as he had fled the scene—oh, how Mike had cursed! For he'd had to accept that when B.J. heard of this she must surely realize that something strange and sinister seemed to be happening here...

Worse, and more recently, there had been a further complication when Mike's monstrous hunger, or more properly his thirst had raged out of control to such a degree that he'd been unable to resist the call of blood. And yet again, probably because The Chemist's rabies strain was running rampant through his system, animal savagery had pushed him over the edge and his victim had died. But at least this time he'd followed the Francezci brothers' precepts in attempting to cover his tracks, except that in his furious passion the method he had used had far exceeded any normal requirement.

And once more cursing his luck, he had stood off in a small group of late-night people on the corner of a street in the red light district, and watched the flames bursting from the window of the squalid room where he'd first drained, then beheaded and set fire to his second dead, never-to-be-undead, prostitute victim. For then—within only a minute or two of the blaze taking hold—some passerby had alerted the night watch at the nearby fire brigade, and a pair of great fire engines had come howling on the scene to fight the fire. The place had been gutted, sure enough, but not before the firemen had dragged the girl's steaming body and severed head free of the inferno…

That had been last night, and this morning's newspapers had carried headline banners of the grisly details, doubtless offering them up as breakfast fodder to B.J. Mirlu and her wine-bar crew. Of course, it was always possible that despite the manner of Mike's attempted disposal of the woman's remains, still B.J. would consider it nothing more than a vicious murder along with the rest of the paper's readers. He could only hope so, for all that he knew any such hope was probably in vain.

For according to the evening broadsheet he'd had delivered to his room, his earlier victim—in mob parlance "that junkie whore"—had after all died some two nights after his attack! And worse: a post mortem was now ongoing, "in order to resolve certain anomalies."

What if anything might such a post mortem reveal, Mike wondered? That something other than drugs had assisted the girl on her way out of this existence? Not at all unlikely.

On the other hand, assuming these events had indeed come to Bonnie Jean's attention and Mike wasn't worrying unnecessarily, she might believe both cases the work of a serial killer—even the same maniac who had followed her girls! Yes, she might *just* think so; but in view of such suspect circumstances that seemed unlikely. For it must be remembered that the Francezci brothers considered B.J. Mirlu "a bitch on the brink of ascendancy," and as such she'd be nobody's fool...

But quite apart from B.J. herself there was someone else—or there *should* have been someone else—who might have turned out to be an additional problem or cause for concern. A shadowy figure whom the Francezcis had warned of in the vaguest possible terms, who yet remained in the back of Mike's mind unknown and unresearched purely because of his absence for the last six or seven days. B.J.'s male companion, yes: if not her lover, or paid minder or hanger-on, then a moon-child thrall and possibly one with limited talents, but in any case a mystery man of whom the twins had known little or nothing other than his existence.

Mike had seen him once only, on the evening of his second day here in the city: a pale unremarkable-seeming specimen who ordinarily he would pass in the street without a second glance. And yet Bonnie Jean Mirlu had stood with him in the entrance to her wine bar, embracing and kissing him before waving him what had appeared to be a lingering goodbye.

Mike had followed some fifty yards behind when the man had walked off down the pavement, entered a side-street and passed from view. But twenty seconds later, on turning the same corner...there had been no sign of the mystery man among the handful of people out walking in the cool evening air; and not far from the corner only one small, late-opening store where he might be browsing. But he wasn't, for even then the storekeeper had been closing up and locking the doors.

Since when nothing more had been seen of him. It was as if he had chosen that evening to disappear, before his place in the scheme of things could be ascertained; which might in the long run be as well. For Mike had arrived at that so-called eleventh hour juncture where he could do without any further problems.

These in the main were his frustrated thoughts, memories that flickered in kaleidoscopic procession through his twisted mind, as he turned from the fly-specked window of his room and prepared to venture out into the gloom of the Edinburgh night. And now more than ever before he could feel the *weight* of time and the immanence of his situation, and knew an enormous sense of urgency! For it must be tonight or at the very latest tomorrow night that he completed the Francezci brothers' task.

But as he stepped out into the darkness he could never have anticipated that in addition to all his self-inflicted problems—and with little more than twenty-four hours to go before The Chemist's poisons were set to complete *their* task on him—tonight would present yet more complications.

For the Necroscope Harry Keogh was also out and about. And not only Harry but someone else: an extremely patient Other who for now and for countless decades past had simply stood off and observed all, but in particular the moon-child, B.J. Mirlu, her pack, and their wine-bar lair.

A sleeper and trusted agent of the Francezcis.

Their watcher...

VIII

That same night, before leaving the wine bar and while talking to young Kate, Harry had glanced through the recently delivered evening paper and had come across an item buried in a back-page column which he'd found both interesting and troubling; either way it was something he would have to look into, and soon.

As for Harry's conversation with Kate: He had enquired not only about the routes the girls took when going to and on leaving the bar, but also their shifts or work rosters. For depending on the number of thirsty customers, B.J.'s with its private members' licence frequently stayed open until the small hours. And the Necroscope's interest had picked up, albeit guardedly, on noting that she, young Kate herself, would be finishing in just an hour's time when Zahanine took over for the late shift.

Harry knew the bar and its precise location well enough; he had long since acquainted himself with many "safe" Möbius coordinates: secure places which he could use covertly to enter into or exit from the general area. But while the bar itself was in a well-frequented road and locale, the districts bordering upon it included several veritable warrens of steep, narrow, cobbled streets and alleyways. Depending on the locations of their various lodgings, most of B.J.'s girls weren't required to navigate the lonelier alleys and would normally keep well away, but for two of them the danger was more or less unavoidable.

In the past, and considering the nature of B.J.'s girls—that they were a new generation of moon-children, lycanthropes descended from the thralls of Radu Lykan, whose werewolf blood had bred true—any risk had seemed minimal and acceptable, but no longer. And now, as a result of B.J.'s concerns, the Necroscope had determined that who or whatever was threatening Bonnie Jean and the pack it was time someone put a stop to it.

For the fact that the unknown assailant had already failed twice in whatever he was trying to do was no guarantee that he would not try again. And as for the identities of his two most likely targets: These were already apparent.

The black girl, Zahanine, was one such, and young Kate herself another. As such, Kate scarcely realized how lucky she had been three nights ago when she'd escaped Mike Milazzo's poisonous bite by the skin of her—or of his?—teeth!

With these things in mind, Harry had distanced himself from the wine bar by a quarter mile and crossed the road into one of his coordinates, the entrance to a narrow alley: as good a spot as any to commence reconnoitring Zahanine's and Kate's routes, searching for the one or two locations on each route which the unknown attacker might find best suited to an ambush.

Then he would have to decide—or perhaps try to discover—which of these locations it would most likely be, and more importantly when. And he must work quickly, for Kate would be leaving the bar in barely an hour's time. She had said she'd take a taxi; but she had also mentioned that after she was dropped off there yet remained a wearying climb to her first-floor flatlet, almost one hundred yards of it up steep stone steps in a narrow canyon-like alley. Once indoors she'd feel safe enough, for the flat was well secured behind "*verra* strong doors wi' guid locks and bolts, aye. It's just a pity the alley's so verra steep and narrow. As for the neighbourhood... well, while it's no a slum it's no of the, er, highest quality, if ye ken mah meanin'."

Harry did indeed "ken" young Kate's meaning; it solved the problem of which locations to reconnoitre first. But before any of that there was someone he must contact about that item which had caught his attention in the evening newspaper. And so, with only a little time to spare, Harry took the Möbius route to his lonely old house outside the city, and from there put through a call to the Night Duty Officer at E-Branch H.Q. in London...

A gangling, ex-intelligence corps major called Fred Madison was on duty. Normally easy-going, and sometimes downright indolent, Madison sat up straighter in his chair and came wide awake when Harry identified himself.

"Harry? Long time no see—or hear. So what's up?"

The Necroscope told him: an item in the Edinburgh Express' late edition. A post mortem that seemed to be returning strange or anomalous results. Some poor girl, a prostitute, had died of drugs, starvation, anaemia; perhaps a combination of all three. Maybe Madison could look into it for him, let him know what was going on?

"Let me look at the screen," the other answered. "Something you think might interest us? I mean, the Branch?"

"I don't know," Harry snapped, and frowned impatiently even though Madison couldn't see him. "Perhaps, perhaps not—but it *does* interest me, and time is pressing..."

And just a few moments later: "Well, what do you know! I've got it on the screen. It must have come to us through the usual channels. Whenever Porton Down is involved we get to know about it first off, er, as you probably know."

Harry's frown deepened. Porton Down: the British Centre for Applied Microbiology and Research. "So, what's going on?"

"Er," Madison seemed of two minds. "Harry, you're no longer with us, right?"

"Listen," said the Necroscope quietly, "I really don't have time for any cloak and dagger stuff. This could be very important to me, you, everybody. So either tell me what you've got on your screen or put me through to Darcy Clarke." Clarke was Head of Branch and had used to be as good a friend as any of Harry's old circle at E-Branch. And after another brief pause:

"Okay, Harry, but I'll need to let Darcy know. It'll be in the situation report in the morning. You do understand that?"

"Of course," Harry answered. "Fine."

"Okay then." Madison sighed, and Harry could sense that he remained reluctant. "Now let's see what we've got here... Well, it doesn't say how the people from Porton Down got onto it, but *their* post mortem has come up with a really weird mixture which includes some drug use and apparent pernicious anaemia—though not enough in itself to have killed her—but the rest of it is...*Jesus!* What in the name of...!?"

"What's that, Fred?" Harry rasped, his impatience mounting. "Something you don't understand? Well neither will I understand if you don't get on with it and tell me what you've got!"

"Harry," Madison replied, "it's not what I've got but what that girl *had!* She'd been sick with several unknown strains of some of the world's nastiest diseases, possibly natural mutations but more likely some weird shit designed in a laboratory! Well, that's according to the Porton Down memo, anyway."

"Diseases? Made in a laboratory?" Shivering, the Necroscope could feel the hairs standing up at the back of his neck. "What kind of diseases, Fred?"

"What kind?" the other came back. "Leprosy, rabies, and—would you believe—the bubonic plague!? *That's* what kind! What the hell is going on up there in your neck of the woods?"

And as suddenly and horrifyingly as that, Harry knew *exactly* what was going on, and he couldn't stop from gasping it out loud, though it was only intended for himself. "He's a plague-bearer!" With which:

Erupting from secret subconscious depths, the Necroscope's metaphysical mind was instantly awash with otherwise forbidden knowledge. He "remembered" everything that Bonnie Jean had told him, and all of it made sense. B.J. Mirlu, a moon-child; likewise her girls—wolflings all—in thrall to a dog-Lord sleeping down the centuries! What better way for her enemies, *their* enemies, to deal with them than by infecting them with the only diseases that could destroy them? Leprosy, the so-called "bane" of both vampires and lycanthropes; rabies, which maddened dogs, causing them to bite and spread it abroad; and the Black Death, the bubonic, a hideous scourge out of the past which even their enhanced systems couldn't handle!

Now the Necroscope understood it all, and in no more than a whisper he said it again: "He's a bloody plague-bearer! A vampire and a plague-bearer!"

"He's a what?" Madison's suddenly anxious voice got through to him. "Who are you talking about, Harry? What's going on?"

But Harry couldn't tell him, and so said, "Nothing, not now that the Porton Down people are on it. I was just...you know, checking things out, that's all." Which sounded stupid, even to him. But Madison wasn't letting it go as easily as that.

"Harry, we're talking about a dead girl here. It's like...I mean, you know—you being who you are, what you are—and if you were wanting to know something about her, like how come you didn't just—"

"Why didn't I speak to her?" Harry cut him short. "Perhaps I would have, if I thought I could get to her, see her without attracting a lot of attention. But this would have been new to her...*death* would have been very new, very terrifying to her. And with those poisons in her—in her body, butchered in the post mortem—asking questions of her wouldn't have been easy. It never is, not for them and not for me..." He gave himself a shake and withdrew from the morbidity of it all, then said:

"Anyway, I've got what I wanted. So thanks." And before the other could say anything else he put the phone down...

Now, with a far more complete picture of all that was happening in his mind, under cover of darkness the Necroscope returned to the entrance of his gloomy alley bolthole near B.J.'s wine bar, and there commenced his previously determined course of action.

Using the Möbius Continuum, he began by making a series of covert jumps that traced Kate's route, as she'd described it to him, all the way from his secret alley to the door of her flat.

And with those locations locked firmly in his mind, he went on to examine Zahanine's routes, accumulating several more coordinates along the way...

At approximately the same time, Mike Milazzo was making his way towards B.J.'s bar intent upon attacking the first of her girls he came across. It no longer made any difference to him whether the attack resulted from an ambush or a chance encounter.

During the past week or so, he had indeed checked out every location or ambush site that the Necroscope was now reconnoitring—both these and some of the routes taken by other members of Bonnie Jean's pack—but the urgency of his mission, not to mention that of his personal situation, was now so extreme that he was on the verge of throwing caution to the wind.

The means of Mike's salvation was in his bite, also in the tiny phials in an inner pocket of his coat; but while the first of these was still viable, the second continued to be an enigma both frustrating and terrifying. Where was the Francezci brothers' sleeper, their so-called watcher? When would he put in an appearance and finally reveal which of the phials contained the antidote? Ah, but Mike already knew the answer to that last...not until he'd completed his task, obviously.

Meanwhile—while yet there *remained* a meanwhile—he found himself salivating or frothing at the mouth more frequently; he felt the seeping stickiness of the pus in his armpits and groin where his clothing adhered, and could even smell it; and insensitive ex-mafioso thug that Mike was, still he was horrified by the rapid, spongy degeneration of his extremities.

Hence his anxiety, his preoccupation as he entered a gloomy alley on Zahanine's route; where even with his heightened vampire senses he failed to note a shadow growing out of the deeper shadows until it was upon him, taking form and confronting him! Momentarily startled, he came to an abrupt halt, his heels skidding on the cobbles. But a moment later, as brute instinct took over, he snarled, lurched forward and reached for the throat of the small man who now stood in his way.

But quick as Mike was the stranger was quicker yet. Without seeming to move a muscle, he yet appeared to flow aside, easily avoiding Mike's reaching hands. And Mike had seen that sinuous, flowing motion before: It belied the little man's appearance no less than it had once belied that of the brothers Francezci! He was—could only be—their man, their thrall, their watcher!

Mike gasped, snatched a breath, took a pace to the rear and hissed his recognition. Then, sighing his relief, he forced his tense muscles to relax as he searched for something to say. But once again the little man beat him to it, and:

"Aye," he said, with a curt nod of his head. "Now ye ken me for sure, d'ye no? Mah name's McGowan. That's *Mr.* McGowan—but ye can call me Angus for simplicity, though it's usually a name Ah reserve for mah friends. As for yeresel': Ah ken yere name well enough, and more than that yere purpose here. But damn me if ye're no a verra sloppy man, Mike Milazzo! And if ye ask mah opinion, when it's doon tae the task in hand ye've been as slow as bleddy treacle!"

Mike's mob nature now surfaced, and he wasn't one to accept insults from anyone, let alone someone of McGowan's small physical stature. "What's that?" he said, scowling and studying the other more closely. "I'm sloppy and slow? Big talk, from a fucking midget!"

"Sloppy and slow, aye." McGowan repeated him. "Not tae mention *forgetful!* Ye might want tae be a wee bit more careful how ye speak tae a body—and in particular *this* body! For Ah'm the one wi' your life in mah hands, am Ah no?"

The darkness of the alley was nothing to Mike and even less to McGowan, and now close-up they continued to study each other. Mike was young, handsome, well-built if not muscular, and close to six feet in height. While McGowan on the other hand—

—Mike might find him laughable, might even be scornful of him, if he didn't know he was a vampire thrall of the Francezci brothers. For Angus McGowan was old, gnarled, and shrivelled as a prune, all five foot four or five of him. Only his nature, of which Mike was now completely convinced, loaned him anything of stature, however illusory. Other than that he was like some kind of living caricature: a "canny" old Scotsman...but his rheumy grey eyes—the eyes of a hawk for all that they were misted—missed very little; and the way his quivering, blue-veined nose sniffed at the air, and at Mike, it must surely be as sensitive as a bloodhound's.

No, Mike finally decided, the Francezcis' watcher wasn't at all someone to be ridiculed. If anything he was impressive, and in his attitude a match for Mike himself. More than a match, as long as he held the key to Mike's future: an extended life or a dreadful death. For as he'd oh-so-correctly pointed out, Mike's continued existence was indeed in his hands.

And now it was as if McGowan could read his mind, which was something else Mike had experienced before, at Le Manse Madonie: the intuitive, near-telepathic talent of long-term vampires, to glimpse the thoughts of others of their kind. And:

"Oh, dinnae fret yeresel', Mike," the little man told him. "Auld Angus has the answer to yere problem sure enough. But Ah cannae gi' it tae ye until the wee job's done—which

Ah'm sure ye ken. But man, yere time is verra nearly up and ye're sick as a body can be. Why, Ah can even smell it on ye… and *in* ye! And when Ah call ye sloppy it's no an insult but a fact."

"How so?" Mike snarled, not knowing what else to say.

"Because Ah've *watched* ye," the other replied. "And Ah tell ye, what may have served ye well in the past in New York is'nae any damn guid tae ye here! Have ye no heard the phrase: longevity is synonymous wi' anonymity? Did the Francezcis no tell ye? *Stealth*, man, that's the word! Now listen:

"Clever men knew it even three hundred and fifty years ago. Aye, and the Francezcis were around even then! Did'nae Descartes hissel' make it clear? Did'nae he say how in order tae live well a body must live unseen? Damn right he did! It was a different season and there were different reasons—religious reasons—but the inspiration was the same: fear o' death!"

Feeling browbeaten, Mike scowled and said, "What? Des who?"

"Hah!" McGowan was scornful. "Sloppy and ignorant too!" And before Mike could reply: "Tae see and no be seen, tae track and no be tracked. Why, ye've a'ready been here—what, eight days is it? And achieved what? *Nothin'* of any value! B.J. Mirlu, she kens there's somethin' in the wind. Her girls are grown more cautious and are sure tae change their tack; as they've done in the past when they've sensed a threat. Ye'll no be catchin' them out so easy the noo. And after a' that ye still seem tae think ye have the right tae take offense when Ah call ye sloppy? *Huh!* Mike, Ah've been here since long before ye were born, and in a' that time B.J.'s moon-children may have spied me once or twice, like a shadow on the wall, or a far faint figure in the nicht—but that's a'. Because Ah watch but Ah'm no watched. Because Ah see but Ah'm no seen. Now d'ye understand?"

Mike had listened in silence; he had heard all and in fact understood all perfectly well. But there was only one thing on his mind, or perhaps two. The first was his horrific condition, and how he must try to find a way not to alienate McGowan, who knew how to alleviate it. And the second was McGowan's criticism; for irrefutable as it was, it nevertheless rankled and he couldn't let it go. And so:

"Yeah, sure I understand. What *you* don't seem to understand is all the shit I've been going through! I know this B.J. bitch is dangerous; if she wasn't the Francezcis would have taken her out long ago, and I wouldn't be here. That's why I've had to be careful, or 'slow' according to you: because she *is* still here. And as for being 'sloppy'—"

"Ah take it ye're speakin' about a couple o' dead yins, are ye no?" McGowan sneered. "Aye, and one without her head, so tae speak? And a' this in the papers under glarin' headlines? So if that's no sloppy maybe ye'll tell me what is! And Ah *do* ken the shit ye've been goin' through. Man, ye *stink* o' it, d'ye no? So now let's walk and talk. We're just a wee bit conspicuous standin' here arguin' in this place."

"What?" said Mike, glancing here and there perhaps a little nervously. "But who's there to see us?"

McGowan likewise peered up and down the alley. And sniffing the night air, he finally nodded his satisfaction; but he nevertheless touched a bony finger to his lips, indicating caution. And then, moving off with Mike alongside: "Aye, who indeed?" he grunted. "But let me remind ye one more time: ye must see, but no be seen. And wi' B.J.'s boyfriend—who or what the bleddy hell he is—that's no easy job. He's like tae appear as if out o' thin air, then disappear like so much smoke! It pains me tae admit it, but Ah've never been able tae track his movements for more than half a mile or so. Oh, he's a queer yin, that yin—a night owl—yet no one o'

B.J.'s pack; and neither kith nor kin to ye and me, if ye take mah meanin'..."

McGowan paused, scowled and shook his head. "So maybe ye've been lucky after a', Mike, that he's no been at B.J.'s wine bar this last week or so. But one thing's sure: he's back the noo!"

Mike nodded. "The Francezcis told me about him, what little they knew! But with all the years you've been here, is that all you've got on him?" It was Mike's turn to sneer. "Maybe I'm not so sloppy after all! But then again, I'm not used to just watching, sneaking about, and doing fuck all else!"

"Oh aye, *verra* clever!" McGowan replied sarcastically. "But ye should ken, Mike, that if Ah'd been telt tae do more than Ah do, be sure Ah'd have taken action long ago, no matter the cost tae mahsel'. For it's no good idea tae fail the Francezcis, and Ah never have. Mah job here has been and still is tae watch and report, that's a'. The fact that Ah'm still here doin' it after a' these years surely speaks for itsel', does it no?"

And before Mike could answer: "Now then, if Ah did'nae ken the brothers' wishes Ah'd no longer be bothered wi' ye; no not at a'. But Ah *do* so ken their wishes. So, d'ye want mah advice or no? Speak up."

Did Mike want McGowan's advice? No, what he really wanted was to take hold of him, bite him, throttle the little bastard and crush his fucking head! But instead he nodded. "Yes, I want your advice. But if I follow it will it work? And will that get me the cure?"

McGowan glared at him. "Do ye no listen tae anythin' a body tells ye? Have Ah no just this minute said how Ah carry out mah bosses' orders tae the letter?"

Again Mike nodded. "Okay, so calm down and advise me."

"Huh!" McGowan grunted. "No so bleddy thick after a' then!" And narrowing his eyes: "Verra well, now listen:

"Ye've been trackin' and attackin' B.J. Mirlu's girls, have ye no?"

"Yes, of course I have," Mike replied and gave a shrug. "In order to transmit these fucking diseases!"

"Aye." And now McGowan nodded. "O' course ye have. But Mike surely the target ye're really aimin' at is B.J. Mirlu hersel', is she no?"

Mike threw up his hands in frustration. "*What?* Sure she is! You know damn well she is! So fucking what? And what the fuck's this for advice? I mean, what are you *getting* at?"

McGowan spat on the cobbles and shook his head in mock pity, "Oh, what a poor blind fool ye are! Blind, aye, because ye dinnae see! Bonnie Jean Mirlu is'nae a lesbian! She does'nae kiss, fondle, fuck, or sleep wi' her girls! She cares for them, aye, but nothin' more than that. And so contact—this fatal physical contact ye're plan calls for—is'nae at a' likely, now is it? Face facts, Mike: there's no way ye can reach this she-wolf through her lassies. Ah, but then there's this English lover o' hers that we've been talkin' about. And—"

Finally Mike saw the logic of it, and barely breathing the words he said: "—And this English guy, this boyfriend?—he *does* sleep with, fondle, and fuck her, right?"

Now McGowan grinned, slowly nodded and replied, "Oh aye, he does a' that, Ah'm sure o' it. And there ye have it."

Mike thought about it, and after a moment frowned and said, "Or maybe not. I mean, if you haven't been able to get near him—and neither have I—then how the hell...? He let the question trail away, but in any case McGowan had the answer.

"Ye're still no thinkin'," he said. "It was never mah intention tae get up close and personal wi' him, only tae see where he goes, what he does. Well, Ah admit Ah failed at doin' that, and Ah still dinnae ken just how he does it; but if the Francezcis had telt me tae kill him, then Ah would'nae have been so fussy or leery. Instead o' hangin' back, tryin' tae follow him and learn his story, Ah would have jumped him and made a quick end o' it. Simple."

Mike nodded. "I see. But they gave you no such orders."

"No. Because as Ah've telt ye they value me too highly as their sleeper and watcher tae let me give mahsel' away, jeopardizin' a position Ah've held for a' these many years. Hah! But is'nae that why they've sent ye? Why o' course it is! And it's also why they've telt me tae advise ye, should ye need it."

"Go on, then," said Mike, nodding. "Get on with it. How do you suggest I get close enough to infect this...this *fucking* disappearing trick of a man? How do I go after him, eh?"

McGowan grinned a sly, evil grin. "Ah, but that's just it. Ye *dinnae* go after him; no, not at a'. Ye set a trap he cannae resist, and let him come tae ye!"

"A trap?"

"Aye. Let him know where and when ye'll be havin' yere fun wi' one o' B.J.'s girls—and be waitin' for him when he comes ridin' tae the rescue!"

"'Let him know that I'll..." Mike frowned. Then, baffled, he shook his head. "But how do I do that?"

"What? Did ye never hear o' the telephone? Listen: What wi' yere previous failed attacks and what a', it's verra possible, indeed likely, that B.J. thinks there's a madman on the loose, chasin' her girls. So now let that selfsame madman call B.J.'s bar—the number's in the book—requestin' tae speak tae a Mr. Keogh. For that's his name, Harry Keogh. At least Ah've learned that much."

Mike's furrowed brow cleared as understanding dawned, lighting up his eyes. "You mean...I get to play some kind of crazy man, right? I talk to this Keogh fuck and threaten one of B.J.'s girls. It will be like I'm calling him out, challenging him. Is that what you're saying?"

"Ah leave a' that up tae ye," McGowan answered, tossing his head in disgust. "What, should Ah do the job for ye mahsel'? Use yere *bleddy* imagination! That's assumin' ye have such!"

Suddenly eager, Mike said, "I'll do it tonight, right now!"

"Now hold!" McGowan cautioned him. "Ah ken how time's narrowin' down, but dinnae be in such a panic that ye trip yeresel' up. Get on back tae yere place and take time tae think it out. Get yere story—everythin' ye'll be sayin' tae him—straight in yere head, and then...tomorrow nicht will be soon enough. Talk tae him durin' the day, makin' yere arrangement for tomorrow nicht, aye. And Ah'll be there when it's done, tae give ye yere reward...*or maybe not,* dependin' how it goes."

"You'll be there?" said Mike.

"Oh aye. Ah'll follow ye, but ye likely willnae see me. For ye ken, Mike, that's how Ah am. It's what Ah do best."

"But—"

"No more buts," said McGowan. "And Ah've spent enough time wi' ye. So Ah'll be leavin' now, until tomorrow nicht. Aye..."

They had reached a junction of alleys. Quick and light as a dancer, the small man spun away into shadows that closed on him like a shroud. Mike stared after him, and even with his vampire eyes had difficulty following McGowan's departure. It was as if the darkness had swallowed him whole; he was there one moment—real and solid as can be—and in another was himself a shadow, merging with those of the narrow alley he flowed into. And like a smudged, shrinking inkblot, McGowan diminished with distance, until finally he flowed vertically up the alley's canyon wall and was gone...

18

Late to bed, the Necroscope Harry Keogh had tossed and turned, sleeping only poorly after Bonnie Jean, vexed at how he'd gone off like that last night without a word of explanation, refused his advances between the sheets. It was only a fit of pique—of which B.J. was as capable as any other woman—and forgotten by the time Harry came awake and found himself forgiven, sucked into her where she kneeled astride him with her breasts tossing within easy reach. But later, when he was up and about, helping with tidying the bar, he blamed his unusual irritability on the fact that she'd rejected him in the night's wee small hours.

Sex was and always had been important to the Necroscope. He was wont to excuse his lustful nature by telling himself it was how he coped with a very different kind of intercourse; for by regular use of this most basic human act, balancing it against his unique ability to converse with the dead, Harry could show himself to be very much alive. The French called love-making—the actual moment of ejaculation—the Little Death, but Harry had always thought of it as the Big Alive! To him it was cathartic, purifying in its insistence that *this* was the real life while his contact with the teeming dead was something else. In short, the sex act assisted in separating, distinguishing, and making acceptable his involvement in two very disparate worlds.

He knew, however, that this was only an excuse, that there was a reason for his irritability other than B.J.'s intransigence in bed last night. It was that his usually accurate intuition in the face of danger would seem to have failed him. For he had actually *felt* the immanence of something—he'd *sensed* it like the tangible heaviness of a gathering storm—and had known it was coming...which it hadn't!

At least, not yet.

Harry supposed he should be relieved that indeed it had not come; but he had been prepared, and now felt off balance. There was a vampire in town, a plague-bearing monster, and last night the atmosphere had seemed tainted with its presence, its threat to B.J., her girls, even Harry himself. Yet this morning, after he had insisted that Bonnie Jean call each of her moon-children individually, all of them—with the exception of Zahanine, who had slept in a small downstairs back room overnight in order to be in early and assist with the cleaning—had been found to be fit and well, safe and sound.

And *then* B.J. had wanted to know why Harry was so concerned when to her knowledge nothing had changed since she'd spoken to him about the possible danger...and furthermore, where had he been last night that he'd stayed out so very late? And what was troubling him now?—for she could sense how irascible he was—and so on.

To which Harry had answered that nothing was troubling him, not really. Maybe it was simply because he'd slept so badly; he was sorry if he seemed a grouch; he would be okay once he'd had a second mug of coffee. As for last night: He had just wanted a little fresh air, and while walking the streets he'd lost track of time.

All of which had apparently, at least temporarily satisfied B.J., and the Necroscope had settled down in an easy chair with a coffee and the morning papers, which he'd scrutinized down to the last dot and dash. He was seeking further information about the murders—especially the results of the post mortem on that poor girl—but was disappointed. There was nothing there, not even a mention. When Harry thought about it, however, it wasn't hard to see why not. If the Porton Down team had released their findings to the press, then at the very least there would have been alarm and despondency among the populace, and at the worst panic in the red-light districts and on the streets.

Harry decided to contact E-Branch again, this time speak to Darcy Clarke himself, but he couldn't do that from the wine bar without Bonnie Jean knowing about it—or *wanting* to know about it; which meant it was time he took another walk. This time she made no fuss: it was a sunny mid-morning after all, meaning it was perfectly safe to be out and about.

Fifteen minutes from the wine bar he found a recessed shop doorway and stepped in…and instantly out again in the front room of his dilapidated old house outside the city—

—Where the phone in its cradle was already ringing! Synchronicity indeed, for it was Darcy Clarke at the other end of the line:

"Harry? Is that you? I mean, of course it is! But I've been trying to get you since eight, maybe nine o'clock this morning. I was just about to put the phone down."

The Necroscope nodded if only to himself, and said, "I know why you're calling. You've been speaking with Fred Madison, and maybe to Porton Down, right?"

For several moments there was silence, and then Darcy said, "Harry, do we need to have people up there in Edinburgh? Do you need our help? I can have a team up there in an hour if necessary. A locator, empath, whatever's required. I suppose what I'm asking: Do you *know* what's required? What's going on, Harry?"

At which Bonnie Jean's post-hypnotic commands at once surfaced, leaving the Necroscope stuck for an immediate answer. For the last thing he wanted was E-Branch involvement in Edinburgh! Locators, empaths—psychics in general—up here? No way! Out of the question!

Harry knew that B.J. and the girls *as individuals* were unusual in that their presence created only very small swirls in the psychic aether—knew that their moon-child nature caused little more than a trace of the telepathic phenomenon known by E-Branch's mentalists as mindsmog—but gathered together as a group in B.J.'s bar, and with espers in close proximity: There would be no escaping the consequences of that! Their immundane signatures would be written clearly on the normally transparent metaphysical void. And:

"No!" he barked, his voice suddenly hoarse.

"No?" said Darcy, sounding puzzled. "Are you okay, Harry?"

The Necroscope coughed to cover his initial knee-jerk reaction, and said, "Excuse me, Darcy, but I've got a bit of a frog in my throat." And after coughing again, as if to clear the imaginary blockage, he went on: "But did you ask me what's going on? Well, that's what I was going to ask you! Have you learned anything else from the Porton Down people? What's their conclusion—that's assuming they have one?"

For a moment there was no answer. Then, still sounding just a little concerned, Darcy said, "Are you sure you're okay?"

"Yes, of course—" Harry answered "—well, with the usual caveats, if that's the right word. But what the hell?—are *you* okay, Darcy? Oh, and by the way: good morning to you, too!"

This sounded more like it: the Necroscope in an assertive, more confident mode, and Darcy's voice at once lost its worried tone. "Quite right, too," he said. "Good morning—and I'm just fine, thanks. With the usual caveats. But you know, Harry, even though it's been a while since we had reason to talk, with shit as ugly as this happening it doesn't leave much time for life's little niceties, now does it?"

"And just how ugly is this shit?" said Harry.

"You mean you don't know?"

"I'm hoping—or maybe not—that you'll corroborate what I *do* know, and what I more than suspect."

And Darcy said: "I understand: It's 'you show me yours, and I'll show you mine' time, right?"

"Something like that," said Harry.

"Okay," said Darcy—fully aware that in the current situation the Necroscope had to be the first best man in the world to whom he should talk—"this is what we've got:

"That first girl they were working on: those poisons they found in her—which is to say those *synthetic diseases*—well that seemed nasty, ugly enough; but there's a footnote. Harry, she'd been bitten on the neck, the jugular, and she was anaemic, missing three or four pints of blood! So then...isn't it true that not so long ago those last two facts, if not all the facts, would have rammed this case right up your, er—?"

"Yes," said Harry. "Right up my, er, alley. And whether or not I like it, that's still very true."

"Obviously, because last night, when all this was breaking, you gave *us* a call! A rare event, which in happier times would have been welcome and much to our liking. But as for right now—well, there you go—I've shown you mine and now it's your turn..."

"Hold on a minute," the Necroscope replied. "You mentioned a *first* girl, so I take it you know about the second girl: the one whose roasted remains were recovered from a burning flat?"

He could sense the other's nod as Darcy said: "I was about to get to that. They're still working on her, but for now it's looking pretty much like the same sort of thing."

"And pretty much as I suspected," said Harry.

"So you *are* on this, then?" said Darcy, his tone making it not so much a question as a matter of fact. And without waiting for an answer: "Of course, at the moment this is all very hush-hush, but we aren't simply sitting on it. I mean, you'll appreciate that we *can't* just sit on something like this!"

Harry was at once alarmed, for B.J.'s sake, but he controlled his surging anxiety and said, "So, what are you doing about it? And whatever that is, I'm hoping it doesn't mean you'll be stepping on *my* toes...does it?"

"Harry, that will have to depend on what you might be about to tell me. But anyway, first let me bring you right up to date with what's happening here at the HQ. For the last half hour or so I've had some of our best people working on it: our locator, David Chung,.empaths, the usual team. But while the actual location is proving difficult, in fact impossible to pin down, the consensus is that there's mindsmog in Edinburgh. It's faint, so faint that it's almost undetectable, and if not for these dead girls turning up—and then Porton Down being on the ball, getting in on it—it's possible we wouldn't even have noticed it. But now that it's come to our attention we know it's definitely there, and that it's mobile, and that's about it. The only good thing about all this—probably—is that you're up there and that you are what you are." Darcy paused for a moment, thinking things through, then went on:

"So, since you're interested in what's going on—maybe to the point of dealing with it?—I find myself of two minds. Do I take a back seat, stay in touch with you, and watch what goes down? Or should I send my team up there so that we can work together on this?"

The Necroscope's anxiety immediately resurfaced, and again he managed to control it. Then, thinking very quickly, he said: "Darcy, since calling the HQ last night I've got much closer to this thing. I think I can probably deal with it but I need some space. And don't get too hung up on this mind-smog thing. Please remember that 'being what I am,'"—he paraphrased what Darcy had said of him a moment ago—"I sometimes have cause to use mindsmog myself. Which is to say I shield my thoughts, deliberately obscuring my psychic and telepathic presence. And if I'm going to deal with this it's a sure thing I'll be doing some of that between now and… and whatever is the outcome. It could get very confusing for everyone if your espers were to get me mixed up with whatever else is out there. Moreover, I'm aware of several entirely innocent 'talents' in my neck of the woods whose psychic signatures would only add to the confusion…"

As Harry paused, Darcy said: "So what you're saying—?"

"—Is leave it to me," Harry answered. "You can tell Chung by all means keep his eye on things, his mind on me, but not to worry about anything else. And he should only *start* worrying if or when I…well, if I were to disappear off his screen."

"Huh!" Darcy snorted involuntarily, then said, "You mean if you were to get yourself killed, don't you!?"

"Hell, no!" the Necroscope instantly replied. "It was just a thought, that's all. No, death is an issue I'll do my damnedest to avoid, probably even more so than other men. Because as you may recall, Darcy, I was there once before—and I didn't much like it..."

The call came just after midday, by which time Harry had been back at B.J.'s for a little over an hour. The day was warm and dry, and the throats of a handful of locals taking their lunch hour break similarly parched, and Bonnie Jean was busy serving drinks with Zahanine while being "chatted up" by their customers. The Necroscope couldn't help but smile to himself, albeit wryly, as he wondered just how eagerly these drinkers would be attempting their various seductions if they knew who precisely they were targeting. It was a thought which—coming from way down deep inside—was at once set aside, forgotten, as B.J.'s post-hypnotic precept came into force, leaving Harry wondering where on earth his mind had been just then!

At which time, as he cleared away and washed empty glasses, the call came.

B.J. picked up the telephone in the bar, spoke enquiringly, frowned and turned to Harry. "It's someone who wishes tae speak tae yeresel'. One o' yere London friends, perhaps?"

And Harry thought: *It could be Darcy at that; perhaps with more news from the Porton Down boffins.* And so:

"It's too busy down here," he told her. "Okay if I take it upstairs?"

"Aye," B.J. answered him, lifting an eyebrow. "Why not? Go on—be just as mysterious as ye like!"

"There's nothing mysterious about it," he replied, shaking his head, leaving the bar and making for the stairs. "I made a few enquiries, that's all. This is probably the answer. Please transfer the call when I pick up the phone, will you?"

In their bedroom he waited until he heard the click as B.J. replaced the handset, then said, "Harry here. That you, Darcy?"

"Harry Keogh?" came a phlegmy, guttural query.

Immediately alert without quite knowing why, the Necroscope narrowed his eyes. But he had sensed something unpleasant, perhaps even threatening, about that throaty, gurgling voice. And:

"Yes," he said. "Harry Keogh, speaking. Who is it, and what can I do for you?"

"Nothing," said the voice. "It's what *I'm* gonna do, and who I'll be doing it to. That and the pain it'll cause you!"

Harry's eyes narrowed more yet. "Who the hell is this?"

"Wouldn't you like to know?" said the unknown other. "But you'll know soon enough. You and that bitch, B.J.—and those tasty, juicy whores of hers. That young one's a real fighter—and she'll need to be when I catch up with her tonight. Except this time I'll know what to expect—and it'll be payback time for that kick in the balls she gave me!"

"You crazy bastard!" Harry growled, as the voice broke out in a spasm of choking, gurgling, almost sobbing laughter.

And then the phone went dead...

His thoughts whirling, straining to fly in a variety of directions simultaneously—picturing in his mind's eye those routes the girls used, especially young Kate's routes, her flat at the top of that steep old alley; but also Zahanine's routes because she, too, had been a target, and this call could well be a ruse to send him stumbling along a false trail—and feeling utterly confused, even to the point of distraction, the Necroscope went slowly back downstairs.

This lunatic…this vampire…this *thing:* he or it knew who Harry was! Not necessarily *what* he was, but definitely who! That must mean something, but what? Was this *really* the work of B.J.'s or her Master's enemies?—(was a thought that surfaced, flitted momentarily across Harry's mind, only to submerge again before he could focus on it)—or was it the Necroscope himself who this creature was targeting, by using B.J. and the girls as a lure? That last hardly seemed likely, for all of Harry's old—and often as not *very* old—enemies were dead…weren't they? Also, this sinister episode had begun while Harry was away from the city…or was that just another component of a clever and indeed bewildering ruse?

"Will ye no tell me what's goin' on?" B.J.'s enquiry, quiet as it was, nevertheless startled Harry as he reentered the barroom. For she had been waiting for him just inside the door to the stairwell, having stationed herself there in order to catch him out, unprepared, as he returned from upstairs. But B.J. had succeeded only in rousing him from his clouded thoughts, his uneasy introspection, and Harry was rarely at a loss when events dictated a rapid recovery.

"Well, as you know," he began, "I've been doing some investigating, and—"

"—Aye," B.J. cut him short. "Makin' a few enquiries, or so ye said. But with whom—if I may ask—and about what? I mean, who can ye possibly talk to, *mah wee man,* about what's goin' on here? For surely ye ken there's things here that ye cannae *ever* speak of! So then, what's yere story, mah brave laddie?"

A moment later, as B.J.'s precepts came into force, if affairs as they stood had been different, impersonal—if anything other than Harry's metaphysical talents, his previous dealings with the undead, or his connection with the espers of E-Branch had been involved—then he would have been obliged to divulge all. But Darcy Clarke and E-Branch had got to Harry first, preceding B.J.'s post-hypnotic commands with orders of their own; by reason of which these mutually conflicting instructions effectively countermanded each other within their own parameters. And for all that this internal conflict was in Harry's subconscious mind—or because it was—he knew little of it except perhaps a certain sense of reluctance: that he must now lie to Bonnie Jean. Wherefore:

"B.J.," he said, "I know very well there are things I can't speak of to anyone—" (A freakish paradox: that Harry could refer to this without being at all aware in his *conscious* mind of exactly what he was talking about, let alone that he was fabricating a story) "—and I haven't and wouldn't. My only thought was to try and discover if you personally were being targeted—you and the girls, I mean, and through you your Master—or if recently there'd been a pattern of similar attacks elsewhere in the land. If the latter, what has happened here might be purely coincidental, and the attacks could be occurring not because of *what* you and your girls are but *because* you are: because you're female, women, and just like any other woman as far as this mad attacker is concerned. Which is why I contacted my old colleagues in London, who have sometimes had to deal with cases almost as strange as this one." (An understatement, that!)

"Police, d'you mean?" B.J.'s voice was sharp now, her Scottish accent falling by the wayside.

"Well, of a sort," said Harry quickly. "Spycatchers, mainly. But really, I can't speak of them…" (How very true; indeed he was *forbidden* to speak of them, no less than of Bonnie Jean herself, or more specifically her nature!)

She blinked, nodded, relaxed a little and said: "So, me and mine—?"

"—Are safe," Harry told her. "At least from my people. But I won't let up from trying to protect you until I'm sure you're safe from everyone and anything. So until this is over and done with—until it's ended, resolved one way or the other—I'll be going out on the streets of a night, looking after the girls as best I can."

And with that, even in his semi-trance condition, with Bonnie Jean's post-hypnotic commands remaining in force, Harry was able to relax a little. He felt a sense of relief that at least the last part of his story, spoken without hesitation, candidly if somewhat robotically, had been the whole truth.

"So then," said B.J., her Edinburgh twang back again, "Yere auld London friends could'nae help ye, eh? But Harry, was it no daft o' ye tae imagine they could? I mean: similar attacks, for *goodness* sake!" And laughing out loud she shook her head. "Just how many rogue vampires do ye think there are in this green and pleasant land, eh?"

Harry stared at her—he stared *through* her with eyes made vacant by her hypnotic commands—and began to speak. "Rogues? Well I can't say about rogues." Again he tried to focus on her, then glanced uncertainly about the barroom. "But there's—"

At which she quickly cut in with: "No, no, *mah wee man!* Ye may forget for the moment what I planted so deep inside o' ye, and answer with a mind that knows nothin' o' that and a voice free o' constraints." For even in her own wine-bar Bonnie Jean wasn't willing to listen to the Necroscope listing the names of her moon-children, or nominating her Master; or for that matter including her own name in any sort of inventory of the undead!

Harry blinked and shook his head; his eyes focussed, and he said, "Yes, you're right: I wasn't thinking. Maybe I was just a bit panicked. I don't like to feel that I or anyone close to me is...well, that we're hunted." And to himself: *For I think of myself more as a hunter than the hunted, B.J.*

And deep inside another voice said: *Yes, and so is she!* But that was Harry's innermost self speaking, and he wasn't permitted to pay attention...

א

This time Bonnie Jean made no fuss when the Necroscope went out into the city. It was shortly after midday, sunny and safe—at least for him, who for all that he didn't much like bright sunlight had no need to fear it—and anyway B.J. knew what he was about: that as best possible he would be seeing to her welfare, on guard against any man or creature intent upon harming her or the pack. And informed by experience, she knew that Harry Keogh was no slouch when it came to looking after people.

Again Harry put the Möbius Continuum to use as he once more checked the girls' routes, ensuring that the coordinates of any especially perilous place were fixed firmly in his metaphysical mind; in particular Kate's route, despite her vow that from now on she would go by taxi. Not that she'd be using a taxi tonight for it was her night off. Still the Necroscope couldn't be sure that Kate would remain in her flat, secure from danger. She was after all a night creature and might decide to venture out; and he couldn't warn her against such a decision in case she or B.J. should ask why—what it was that Harry feared?—which in its turn might well jeopardize his position in the scheme of things by leading to another bout of hypnotic interrogation.

But the fact remained that if Kate *did* venture out—even were she to phone for a taxi—still she couldn't be picked up from or delivered to her door; not in the steep, narrow, canyon-like alley where her flat was located. No, she would be obliged to walk: either to continue on up the alley to some street at a higher elevation, or down one hundred yards or so, and an equal number of time-worn stone steps, to the road at the foot of the alley. And right there—in that poorly lit, high-walled brick tunnel of a place where the terraced dwellings crowding on both sides were often as not unoccupied, their windows and doorways boarded up—that was the most likely spot for an ambush…

Dwelling on such things as he went about his self-imposed duties, Harry could scarcely fend off an involuntary shiver as he stepped from the Möbius Continuum into the alley in question and pictured such an attack on young Kate. Oh, Kate was a moon-child and therefore scarcely innocent in any sense of the word, but she was also vulnerable. And for that matter, who wouldn't be vulnerable against the toxic and undoubtedly lethal bite of this vampire terror? It was horrible to contemplate the effect such a bite would have on Kate, a creature the Necroscope had come to think of simply as a pretty young girl.

On the other hand—quite apart from not wanting to explain his concerns to Kate or Bonnie Jean for fear of somehow revealing his sources—there was another very much darker reason why Harry might find it self-defeating to reveal the nameless maniac's threat: simply that it could be as well to let things run their course, using Kate as a lure to draw this plague-bearing lunatic into a trap—even though no such trap had as yet been devised!

The Necroscope didn't care for that last idea—or that he was even considering it despite that he was!—and as he made a Möbius jump from a shaded doorway to the higher level where the entrance to Kate's flat lay in a shallow recess beneath an old brick archway, he once more felt the preternatural chill of an involuntary shiver.

But no, it were best to look on the bright side (Harry told himself) and assume that Kate would stay indoors tonight; which considering her recent scare was still the most likely contingency. And if she did, how then might this unknown plague-bearer get to her in the safety of her own place?... Kate's very own, very lonely place...

And now he was there at the place in question, or at least its entrance; where, in the black brick wall at the rear of the recessed area under the arch, a pair of narrow, iron-clad doors stood side by side. The door on the right had a single bull's-eye window, dusty and fly-specked; looking in, Harry could only just make out an empty, gloomy passageway extending into impenetrable shadows. This wasn't Kate's door, for he remembered her saying that she lived upstairs, on the first floor.

Turning to look back down the alley, Harry saw that no one was in sight. Putting his ear to Kate's door, and hearing nothing of activity from within, without further pause he conjured a portal of his own, stepped through it *and* the real door both, and stepped out again on the other side, *in*side the building.

Now the Necroscope stood at the foot of carpetted stairs in a narrow stairwell that was clean and free from dust; and there too he immediately detected the faintest trace of Kate's favourite perfume, by which he was doubly assured that the stairs led to her first-floor accommodation.

She would be up there even now, of course, for despite that she was as much or more moon-child than vampire, still it would be no easy matter for her to venture out into broad, sunny daylight. Under a heavy parasol and wrapped as for winter it would be possible but uncomfortable to say the least—not to mention very dangerous. Far better to stay indoors, at least until sunset.

There was a light switch which Harry couldn't use for fear that it might illumine not only the stairwell but some room in the flatlet overhead, which would surely draw attention to his presence; but in a little while, when his eyes had grown accustomed to the dimness of the place, he was able to see an inner door on a landing at the head of the stairs. A Möbius jump took him to the landing where he stepped forth without a sound immediately outside the stout door. The door had several brass keyholes marked with the scratches of constant use; and Harry felt sure there would be good strong bolts on the inside, even such as Kate had mentioned.

Finally the Necroscope was satisfied that he need go no further. The picture in his mind of a diseased, therefore weakened vampire—a creature which Kate had already fought off on one occasion—didn't really permit of such a monster breaking down doors as strong as these in order to get at her. Wherefore if young Kate stayed home tonight she was surely safe; in which case, how would the sick monster react finding that she was unavailable, his threat unworkable? Would he simply change his plans to suit and move on to another girl, perhaps Zahanine?

With which questions nagging at his mind, Harry conjured a Möbius door and transferred to the alley's ancient stone flags in the shade of the wall over the arched entry.

And from there, for the moment going on foot, he stepped out thoughtfully down the time-hollowed stone steps, and pondered his next move.

And behind him, upstairs in her flat, young Kate was struck by a sudden wave of unease—a feeling of persecution, perhaps? Of invasion or violation of spirit. And if Harry had chanced to look back just then, he might have noticed a slight movement of the heavy drapes at a single window on the first floor: a sliding window with a single pane of glass, behind a narrow balcony that was little more than a railed ledge. And if Kate had been looking down into the alley instead of gazing out over dreaming Edinburgh, frowning inside at these feelings of gathering immanence, she might have seen Harry as he paced from dazzling sunlight into deep shadow and didn't step out again...because he was no longer there.

But no, she could only stand to look out on such brilliance for a second or two, following which the curtains twitched back into place again and both Kate and Harry went about their businesses unobserved and mutually unaware...

The afternoon passed; evening came on; soon the velvety dusk of summer was settling on the city. To Bonnie Jean's surprise Zahanine came in early...while it wasn't her shift she'd felt out of sorts, fidgety at home; she would be more at ease serving in the bar. Fine by B.J., who was more than grateful, for Margaret McDowell, another of her moon-children, had called in sick; and for more reasons than one it also worked out well for the Necroscope. He wouldn't have to supply an excuse for not offering to help in the bar—which meant he would be free later to venture out into the night—and at the same time it narrowed down the plague-bearer's choices further yet.

With Zahanine out of harm's way, and young Kate safe behind stout doors, who was left for the diseased madman to target? Of course, Kate, Zahanine, and Margaret weren't Bonnie Jean's only moon-children. Her pack—the wine-bar staff—was made up of those already mentioned plus two more girls: a willow-slim redhead by the name of Sandra Mohrag, and her raven-haired cousin, Moreen McNiven. These last named shared a house out toward Dalkeith in a well-lit, heavily populated area. But the Necroscope knew they used taxis in the main and normally worked the bar as a team; they enjoyed each other's company, and anyway there was safety in numbers. To check their taxi routes along Edinburgh's main thoroughfares would serve no purpose; even if they went on foot Harry would think it highly unlikely that there would be a single ideal spot for any kind of ambush along those routes.

Also, he found that try as he might he couldn't ignore that certain sick, phlegmy, threatening voice in his head, that kept repeating itself about young Kate being, "A real fighter—" And how she would need to be, "—when I catch up with her tonight!"

Always it came back to that: tonight. And also to Kate, who despite all Harry's fears was perfectly safe at home tonight—

—Wasn't she?

As night drew in, Bonnie Jean sensed the Necroscope's preoccupation, his agitation, and asked him: "So then, what's wrong the noo, Harry? What's on yere mind?"

"I think I'll be going out a little later," he answered her at once. "I'm not happy that everything is alright. I'm feeling as fidgety as Margaret, unsettled, uncomfortable."

B.J.'s eyes narrowed immediately, and she lowered her voice to enquire: "Oh, and is it this business with the murderer, *mah wee man?* But have ye forgotten what he is; how dangerous he is? No—" and she shook her head, "—it's no a good idea tae be out on Auld Windy's streets in the dark o' the nicht, Harry."

"I know," he answered, "but better that than being in here, worrying about your girls out there!"

Then, as if his reply had flown right over B.J.'s head, she reached out to stroke his face, nodded and said, "Aye, and it's been makin' ye itch ever since we spoke o' it at length, has it no?"

"Of course it has," Harry replied. "There's a madman on the streets, a vampire, an indiscriminate murderer who doesn't seem concerned that he leaves this...this *bloody* trail of evidence behind his kills and makes little or no effort to clean up after himself. He's...he *has* to be crazy, B.J.! He's a *menace* and a threat to all of us, especially to you and the girls! And knowing that he's..." Harry paused again, "out of control—out of his mind—well, I can't simply sit around twiddling my thumbs, doing nothing about it."

Twice in a mere handful of words the Necroscope had almost said: *"He's a plague-bearer, B.J.!"* But he couldn't; there was that in his mind which simply wouldn't allow it. It contravened Darcy Clarke's post-hypnotic precepts, insofar as he might then need to explain just exactly how he *knew* they were dealing with a diseased thing—which was *because* E-Branch had told him so—which in its turn was also because his old friends in that most secret of intelligence agencies had a legitimate interest and a huge down on all such creatures...indeed a mandate to destroy them. Which would of course include B.J. and her moon-children!

But in any case Harry's confusion had escaped B.J.'s notice. And sighing resignedly, she stroked his face again, dropped her Scottish accent and said, "Don't for a moment think I don't appreciate what you're trying to do for us, Harry. But honestly, I worry about you just as much and perhaps more than you do about me and mine. I know that you're a very strange—maybe I should say very different—sort of man, Harry Keogh; also a very capable one. Nevertheless you *are* just a man, and if anything were to happen to you..."

"But it's not going to," said Harry, shaking his head as he sensed her post-hypnotic spell fading. Her heart hadn't been in it this time, apparently. It was possible she was of two minds; maybe she realized her best bet would be to have him out there, her champion against the night's unknown dangers. Well perhaps, but B.J. wasn't about to confess to vulnerability—not even to herself. Nor was she quite ready to give in to him. Wherefore:

"Harry, now listen—" and giving it a last try, she reached under the bar for a very special bottle, "—surely you know how much happier I'll be if you'll stay here, safe indoors with me? Now wouldn't you rather do that: have a glass or two of my good wine, maybe—" she showed him the bottle, "—and stay here with me?"

What, a glass of B.J.'s special wine? No way, not a hope in hell! Not tonight Bonnie Jean! One glass of that positively addictive stuff: The Necroscope knew he would be no good for anything, that he'd be lucky if he could make his way upstairs to bed unaided!

And so, again shaking his head in denial, also to clear it of mental fluff, he focussed his eyes, stared at B.J. and said: "No, I don't think so. I'll need to have my wits about me, B.J., if I'm to be going out."

"But Harry, I really don't think—"

"But I do!" He cut her short. "Not right now, but later I *will* be going out."

At which, seeing the strength of his will, also his dedication—his love, perhaps?—she simply accepted it, nodded and said no more…

Checking routes that he had already checked more than once, the Necroscope found a small measure of relief in keeping busy; but at the same time he realized the futility of his activity. Knowing or regarding with suspicion half-a-dozen locations where an attack might happen didn't help him, couldn't tell him at which of them—if any—it would definitely be, nor when exactly it *might* be. Moreover, there was a real and significant measure of danger in what he was doing, in this task for which he'd volunteered himself. For despite that he always took care when using the Möbius Continuum—even when doing so under cover of darkness—still he risked being seen either entering or departing from what was (except to Harry himself) a conjectural, mathematical dimension. And such a sighting would be bound to arouse a great deal of inconvenient curiosity.

Also, and frustratingly, while as a means of conveyance the Continuum was swift, indeed instantaneous, still the Necroscope couldn't be in two or more places simultaneously. And meanwhile something deep inside, which felt like something from *outside*—by now an almost familiar sense of dark and deepening imminence born perhaps of his keenly intuitive nature, but just as likely of simple commonsense—was telling him that he shouldn't even try to cover every possible eventuality, because there was only one place where he would really need to be.

And as the seconds ticked relentlessly by, becoming minutes and then hours, he began to realize where this futility he felt had its source, and where it was leading him: in the constantly growing conviction that the one place where he really *had to be*—and then at the right moment—was with the one person he was still most concerned about: namely young Kate.

Safe at home, was she? Well, maybe. But alone at home, definitely. And in Harry's head, louder by the minute, always that phlegmy, guttural voice whose sick laughter more than hinted of sobbing; that voice telling him—

—That young one's a real fighter…And she'll need to be when I catch up with her tonight…Payback time for that kick in the balls she gave me.

But apart from the telephoned threat, which could of course be an empty one, what other evidence was there that Kate was in harm's way?

Still hesitant, torn two ways, Harry pondered the question. Well she *had* been the victim of an attack, albeit a failed one, hadn't she? Perhaps the diseased maniac knew that Kate would be home tonight and was counting on it. Perhaps he'd been watching her, studying her routines…and perhaps he still was.

With regard to that last possibility or theory, that Kate's routines were even now under close scrutiny, it dawned on Harry that he had at his disposal a means of positively confirming or invalidating the worrying notion—and without wasting any more time at that. And so Harry finally decided: that right or wrong he must for the moment concentrate his efforts on Kate, who remained the youngest and most vulnerable member of the pack…

Now there were other things to decide; namely the where and the when of it.

The where: Kate's flat would be the obvious starting point, and Harry knew the coordinates. He went there—at least as far as a "place" in the Continuum which corresponded to the landing on the stairs outside Kate's inner door—but as soon as he got there, which was at once, he simply floated in Möbius darkness, the *utter* darkness of a place before time, making no attempt to conjure a door or to exit from the Continuum at that location.

It was proximity that mattered: the fact that Kate had been here. Not how frequently she had been here; only the *last* occasion that this spot had known her presence. For that was where, and when, Harry would make his connection with her without that she would ever suspect that he had been here. Because while the Necroscope could not be with Kate in real time, he nevertheless knew how to connect with something of her in Möbius time.

"Time," yes: That was the essence of his plan.

For not so long ago (while yet it often felt like decades!) the occasion had arisen when Harry had plumbed past and future time in the search for his wife and son. And on one such occasion he'd seen the scarlet life-thread of a vampire crossing his son's pure blue thread in the Möbius time-streams. Now he would use Möbius time again, this time to track Kate's life-thread.

But first he must find that life-thread.

So when was Kate last here on this landing? Last night most probably, on arriving home after paying her taxi fare and climbing the alley's stone steps from the street to the outer door, and then the stairs to this landing. So that and then was where and when he must go: back to last night.

And yet...Even now the thought of Möbius time-travel gave Harry pause. This first leg would not be problematic, he knew; for the past, even the recent past, was over and done with; it contained nothing worth fearing, for nothing could be changed. But as for the future...

The future was ever a devious thing, and the last thing the Necroscope wanted to witness was his own blue life-thread suddenly extinguished, signifying his extinction and, by his reckoning, his premature membership in the Great Majority! While that would surely happen one day, because no one is immortal, he was naturally anxious to avoid a preview of that unfortunate inevitability. In short, he didn't want to know when.

But that was for the future while Harry's immediate concern was in the past. His hesitation had lasted only a moment (which was no time at all in the Möbius Continuum) before he found and opened a past-time door. And there it was, the achingly brilliant past of humanity: a myriad blue life-threads receding, narrowing down and finally (or initially?) coming together, converging in the two-and-a-half-million years distant blue core which was mankind's beginning.

Though Harry had seen it often enough before, still his jaw fell open as he stared and stared...and *listened!* For despite the absolute quiet, the utter absence of sound, it was as if he heard something: an angelic chorus—an orchestrated, interminable *Ahhhhhhhhhh!* A mystical, massed sighing consisting of one continuous note that existed solely in the Necroscope's imagination, sounding only in his unique mind—for he knew that time was as silent as the Continuum itself. Of course it was; for if all the sounds of the past were given voice here, that would be an unbearable tumult.

One of the pure blue life-threads beyond the past-time door issued from Harry himself; it was the trail that he'd left, and continued to leave, in past time; and he compared it to the jet exhaust of an aircraft thrusting him into the future, where the invisible door in which he had anchored himself was in fact the present or more properly an interface between The Past and What Was Yet To Be. But Harry's life-thread was just one of uncountable others.

He leaned forward, glancing this way and that, up and down; until just beyond the door something more of the interface, the vast, ever-increasing canvas of past-time became visible—but never the entire width of the present, and no glimpse of course of the future. That was for later.

"Later."

The word or thought spurred Harry on, for time was "narrowing down." A malapropism, of course, because time like space is ever expanding. Putting that thought aside, Harry launched himself headlong through the past-time door and fought against the opposing current. Simultaneously, he watched his life-thread as it appeared to wind itself back into him, while also seeming to reel *him* back into the past! And moving in opposition to time's flow, he held his wrist to the fore with the face of his wristwatch visible in the blue glare of his life-thread. And there a truly astonishing sight: the second hand blurring as it hurtled anticlockwise round the dial, the minutes in a crazy whirl, and the hours unwinding like so many seconds! Harry supposed it was possible that he too was somehow growing younger: a notion that had never occurred to him before. Since his memory appeared unaffected, however, and he didn't intend to retreat too far into the past (and by no means permanently) he likewise supposed, or more properly hoped, that it would make no great difference.

Whichever, Harry let time's opposing thrust slow him down, which also served to slow the frantic activity of the hands on his watch. It had been almost eleven-thirty *tomorrow* night when he commenced this experiment; but now, in "no time at all" (yet another notion to set his senses spinning!)

already it was midnight on the previous night. And he slowed himself more yet.

Eleven-thirty...eleven...ten-thirty...and finally ten o'clock last night, when at last—

—There she was! That pale pink life-thread which was young Kate, coming nearer and even seeming to encroach upon him where she came out through her door and onto the landing. He couldn't see her in the flesh, only the pale pink life-thread of a moon-child—a creature by no means undead because she'd never been dead—but he could imagine her, picture her walking *backwards* down the stairs, not only on her own Earthly, three-dimensional plane but also in his Möbius time; which "for the moment" meant time in reverse, "naturally...?"

But these were confusing thoughts which Harry must put out of mind, concentrate on what he was doing, and watch over Kate. Which meant that now too he must turn about face and let time's onrushing tide carry him back toward the **Now.** Except that being almost a day in arrears, he must needs travel faster than time. And reversing his direction, he *willed* himself forward; for the Necroscope had long since learned that in the Möbius Continuum, where even the smallest electrical impulses of vacuous thoughts have weight, the force of will is a physical concept also.

As Harry moved back toward the future his Continuum coordinates remained coincident with the landing outside Kate's door; and this way he could be satisfied that she was indeed home...which she *would* be in just another moment.

And right now (or then) here she came: Kate's lupine life-thread once again swerving toward him as he pictured her climbing the stairs exactly as she had done last night, entering her flat, and locking the door behind her. But even though Kate had now drifted somewhat apart from him, still her thread was visible nearby as time propelled them back towards their **Now.**

So that when the hands on Harry's watch began to slow down again, released from their hurtling forward motion to resume an everyday pace, he knew he had returned to the interface: to the past-time door where his motion was held to a constant rate of one second per second. And without pause he carried on through the door into the Möbius Continuum's "ordinary" plane of being and the **Now.**

There in the absolute nothingness, floating in weightlessness, Harry paused to give thought to what he'd learned or achieved, if anything. Well he knew that for more than twenty-four hours since last night Kate had remained indoors; her pink life-thread was close by even now; it had swung only marginally here and there while she performed this or that task within her flat. Also, in all the time the Necroscope had spent in Kate's vicinity, at no time had he been aware of any crimson life-thread or threads—the sure sign of a vampire or vampires—encroaching upon, coming close to, or lingering anywhere at all near Kate's. In fact, and apart from the pale pink stain of her own essence, as far as Harry could tell the past-time lanes had been totally free of vampire influence, at least in her locality. Indeed, he had seen nothing whatever of crimson activity.

And as for the time now...he glanced at the luminous dial of his watch: It was a minute or so prior to eleven-thirty p.m. He was back when he'd started out.

Night time—indeed the middle of the night, almost—and Kate was apparently safe, alive and well, and so far completely unthreatened. Harry was naturally glad for her sake... and yet in a way he was also disappointed. For it was beginning to look like his instincts—subverted and sidetracked by that phlegmy, sobbing voice on the telephone—had on this occasion led him astray.

But despite that the Necroscope felt flat and partly spent, with his previous sense of imminence and urgency fast dissipating, still he was determined to see it through: to follow the course he had set himself to its conclusion and see what would or probably would not now transpire.

For which reason he sought out a future-time door...

XI

Just seven minutes away in time to come, and a little less than fifty yards from the ground floor entrance to Kate's flat, Mike Milazzo made his way like an outsize garden snail up the canyon alley's worn stone steps. Mike was aware that his trousers were damp at the waist and down the legs, where dribbles of the vile fluid that his body was leaking gathered or ran in slow streamlets; and he knew his shoes were full of the stuff, which squelched and brimmed over as he walked or hobbled, leaving a silver snail-trail that shone in the light of a gradually waxing moon.

Also, his gums had shrunk back, his teeth had loosened, and he constantly licked at the froth as it dried on his lips, spitting it out along with endless blobs of the thick yellow phlegm that flooded his mouth from some seemingly inexhaustible source. Worst of all, Mike could *smell* himself: the unmistakable stench of decay, of a body fast rotting alive!

And yet, even though almost all hope was gone and the true death loomed ever closer, still Mike's stubbornly human streak—plus the enhanced physical powers of an undead vampire—sustained him. And even in the delirium of onrushing devolution he imagined himself buoyed up, almost weightless; and despite that he limped up the alley, still he felt that he flowed! And his hatred of the Francezcis, of The Chemist in his Bulgarian laboratory, and most recently of Angus McGowan: all of this pent-up loathing floated uppermost in what remained of his disintegrating mind.

Angus McGowan, yes, and his lying promises. Where was Angus now? Nowhere to be seen. And Mike's awareness of the tiny vials in his pocket so keen and constant that it caused them to weigh like lead. Should he take them anyway? Take the contents of all three, regardless of the outcome? Was there still time? But how could *any* antidote possibly fight off the horror that had overcome him? And where was the one who was supposed to advise him?

"McGowan, you rotten little bastard!" Mike hissed the words out through a fresh burst of froth. "You said you'd be here...argh! *Argh!*...but where the fuck are you?"

That last was like an invocation.

A dark shadow seemed to grow out of the brick wall's deeper shadows directly in front of Mike, bringing him to a staggering halt. It was Angus McGowan, his eyes ablaze in the night, feral in their reflection of a stray moonbeam's faint yellow gleam.

For the merest moment startled, Mike just as quickly recovered. But this time his instincts, reflexes, and especially his loathing, would not be denied. He was no sooner confronted than he grabbed the lapels of McGowan's long black coat and drew him close.

McGowan turned his face from Mike's foul breath and gasped: "Mike, Ah heard what ye whispered—*and* what ye were thinkin'! But here Ah stand, even as Ah telt ye Ah would. So then, have Ah no kept mah word?"

"Too late! Too *late!*" Mike gurgled, tightening his grip for all that certain of his twig fingers felt they might break off. "Are you blind? Can't you see I'm—*argh!*—finished?"

"Never, never!" The little man cried. "By tomorrow's sunup, then ye'd be done for, aye. But tonight there's still time!"

"Which vials do I drink from? And how, in what order?" Mike coughed the words out. "There are three different colours."

"Aye, so Ah'm informed—red, black, and yellow. But Mike, what o' the job? The job's no done, man!"

"The job?" Mike brought up phlegm, spitting it aside before continuing. "The—ach, *argh!*—fucking job? I'm fucking *dying!* The true death, you little—*argh!*—little bastard!" He pressed McGowan to the wall, breathed into his face. And the little man saw his wet mouth gaping, saw the pus gathering in his eyes and read his mind. But:

"If ye do that—" he cried, "—what ye're thinkin', then it really is over!"

Mike nodded, closed his awful mouth, and said: "For both of us, Angus. It'll be over for *both* of us. Because even if I knew how to use the antidote, there's not enough of it for two, only for one. And however it went I wouldn't be giving any to you!"

"But there's still time for ye, Ah swear it! Only let me go and Ah'll help ye. Ah'll see ye through it!"

Now Mike saw that he had the upper hand—at least for the moment. And so: "Job or no job," he choked and gurgled, "you'll tell me what I want to know right now or I'll bite your fucking face—*argh!*—and feed slop into the wounds. And just to make sure, I'll cough up some of this shit into your mouth, too! And in another week or so, maybe ten days, when you've been through what I've been through—then you'll follow me down into hell!"

But at that, amazingly, Mike sensed McGowan's resolve stiffening; and in confirmation of this notion the other gasped: "Ah cannae believe ye'd do it, no while there's a chance ye'll come out o' this alive!"

Mike nodded, smiling however monstrously. "Oh, really? You think I won't do it? Then tell me, you little shit, what have I got to lose? Oh, *ha-ha-ha!"* He uttered a harsh, mad laugh, then quickly sobered and said: "Well, that's it. You can kiss all of this goodbye, Angus." With which he opened his mouth more yet.

And finally McGowan broke. "Verra well, Ah'll tell ye!" he gasped, averting his face once again from Mike's gaping, frothing jaws. "Show me the vials. Quick now; for the sooner ye take it, the sooner it'll work on ye."

"It?" Mike gurgled, continuing to press McGowan to the wall and holding on to him with one hand while groping in his inside pocket with the other. "Don't you mean them?"

"It or them: what's the difference?" McGowan snapped, wriggling in Mike's grip. "Ah mean the antidote! Dinnae quibble the noo, Mike! Just show me they bleddy vials."

Easing the container out of his pocket, Mike used his thumbnail to free the catch. The lid opened slowly on lightly sprung hinges, revealing the three vials. And:

"Aye," said McGowan, peering at the tiny glass bottles and nodding his head eagerly now, "that's it sure enough—the red, black, and yellow."

"Again with the 'it,'" said Mike. "What's going on, Angus?"

Nodding again, and avoiding the froth that flew from Mike's foaming, belching mouth, the other said: "Ah'll tell ye in just a second. But first—maybe ye'll tell me how ye intend tae do it."

"Eh? How I'll do what?"

"Why, how ye'll get intae the wee girl's place, o' course!"

"The girl?" Mike's mind was drifting.

"The job, man!" McGowan snapped. "The bleddy job! For if ye dinnae finish it, what use tae live with the Francezcis huntin' ye down tae the ends o' the earth? And by now Ah'm certain sure ye ken there's more and worse ways tae suffer the true death."

"The girl," Mike mumbled again, trying to focus his mind.

And McGowan said, "Ye cannae just ring her bell or knock on her door. And it's likely that B.J.'s bleddy white knight is up there the noo, baby-sittin' the wee bitch and waitin' on ye!"

In Mike's mind the facts of what was happening drifted back into focus. He felt his hand trembling, and in fear of dropping the container snapped it shut single-handed and slipped it into a side pocket. Then, while again using his body and both hands, as before, to restrain McGowan—and for all that he longed to savage, crush, and kill him—still Mike was able to recognize the awful truth and logic of the little man's warning about the nature of Francezci revenge...

For which reason he struggled with himself, was able to put aside his own vengeful urges and answer McGowan's earlier question:

"I don't—*arghhh!*—I don't fucking *know* how I'll get in! Maybe...maybe I can break in?"

McGowan wriggled again, tried to shake himself loose, shook his head instead and said: "What, in yere condition? Oh, there's still a thing or two that ye *can* do, for sure; but break doon a sturdy door? No way, laddie! Yet even now Ah tell ye there *is* a way in! Only look up there, where mah gaze directs ye."

And turning his head and feral yellow eyes as far as Mike's grip would allow, the little man stared some fifty yards up the alley's dark canyon throat, focussing on a feature in an otherwise blank brick wall no more than ten or eleven feet above the arched-over lower entrance to Kate's flatlet.

Blinking a mucous film from his eyes, Mike followed McGowan's gaze to a lone window with a railed balcony that was little more than a ledge. And despite the poisons, the lethal diseases that had ripened in him, still in command of a vampire's night-vision the ex-Mob thug could see well enough—even as McGowan had seen—that on this balmy summer night young Kate had left her window standing ajar. A lace curtain stirred and fluttered, letting in a cool night breeze...where in all likelihood, and very soon, the same window would let in something far more substantial than a breeze, though by no means as natural and harmless...

Glancing at McGowan, Mike's look framed a question to which he already knew the answer. And:

"Aye," said the little man, nodding a confirmation. "Now ye see it: yere way in. And if B.J.'s English lover is in there... then the job's as good as done. What d'ye say tae that?"

"I say—" Mike gurgled, "tell me about the antidote—and consider yourself lucky to go on living! Maybe then I'll get to the job."

"Oh, ye stubborn bastard!" McGowan moaned. "But verra well, have it yere own way. Ah'll tell ye—for it's a fact that yere time is runnin' out. Are ye ready with the vials, then?"

And holding McGowan with one hand, Mike once again took out the small metal case and opened it.

The little man nodded and said, "Go on then: first take the yellow yin and drink it tae the dregs, every wee drop."

Mike faltered, blinked, gurgled and finally said: "The yellow one? Are you sure? What, and no 'wee tricks,' Angus?"

"None whatsayever," McGowan shook his head. "For if ye fail ye'll no be alone in yere troubles; they Francezcis dinnae tend tae look too kindly on anyone who fails them, and that includes their agent and so-called Watcher, aye!"

The little man's words with their ring of sincerity sparked a fresh burst of hope in Mike; whatever the outcome, he felt he couldn't afford any further delay.

Using his bulk to keep McGowan pinned to the wall, and both hands to remove the yellow vial, then close the case and slip it back into his pocket, he unstoppered the tiny bottle and tilted its contents into his eager throat. Then, trembling and jerking to the shock of the liquid going down—which, while it lasted only a second, was not unlike the eye-watering sting of an ice-cold beer, or maybe the burn of a fiery liquor—Mike gulped at the night air, blinked…and staggered a very little.

But a little was all the opportunity that McGowan needed!

He slid sideways away from Mike, then continued to slide *up* the wall! And facing outwards, flat against the wall—with the palms of his hands, his narrow shoulders, back and buttocks appearing to act like a gecko's adhesive pads—McGowan slithered or climbed until he was well beyond Mike's reach; where finally he paused to look down at him and grin.

Mike snarled, raising his hands as if to snatch at McGowan; but laughing softly and light as a feather the other climbed to an even higher elevation, from where he called down:

"Now think, Mike, think! Auld Angus isnae the one ye should be chasin' after! And look here now: am Ah no showin' ye one o' they things Ah said ye could do? And so ye can, because ye're a vampire no less than mahsel'—just a wee bit less experienced, that's a'. But still Ah'm sure that if ye'll only gi' it a try, then ye'll see just how right Ah am. Only don't go wastin' yere time thinkin' tae chase after me. The wall ye *should* be climbin' is a wee bit further up the alley."

"But the antidote!" Mike choked, coughed, spat on the stone steps. What's the—*arghhh!*—point without the antidote, you cheating little bastard!?"

"Oh, that," said McGowan, with a careless shrug. "The antidote, is it? The red and the black, d'ye mean? Well, what are ye waitin' for? Go on then: take 'em. Drain 'em tae the dregs!"

"What?" Mike gasped, afraid and bewildered. "Take *them?* But which one do I leave out? Which one will kill me?"

Again McGowan's callous shrug and his look of total indifference. "Take *both* o' them," he said, "whichever way ye fancy!"

Mike had meanwhile taken out the case again. Opening it, he stared at the remaining vials as if hypnotized. And: "Take both of them." He repeated the little man's incomprehensible instructions. And again: "Both of them? But—"

"There's no 'but' ye great fool!" McGowan cut him off. "The Chemist only telt ye what he was told tae tell ye! Aye, and mahsel' likewise. Three colours for three sicknesses, and each one an antidote in its own right! But dinnae think tae ask me which is which for Ah dinnae ken! And anyway what odds? Just take 'em however ye like, and have done wi' it."

"Jesus *Christ*!" Mike spat the words out, along with a great blob of phlegm. "Why you cheating, black-hearted—ach! *Argh*!—little *bastard*!"

But then, since there was nothing else for it—and because he was almost past caring—he drained the tiny bottles "to the dregs," first the red and then the black...

The liquids stung going down, at which he believed he could actually feel them working!

"O' course ye can!" said McGowan, reading his mind. "Ye'll feel light in both yere head and yere limbs; light as a bubble, as if ye were floatin'! That's how it is for each and every one o' us—o' our kind, Ah mean—but more especially in times o' danger, such as this. The closer tae death, the more the vampire in us fights back."

That last would seem to be true enough, for as before Mike fancied himself buoyed up. He felt weightless yet potent—in a state of transition, of metamorphosis—enabled and capable, even of aerial flight! But:

"Ah no, not just yet!" said McGowan, chuckling. "Ye'll no fly, Mike, but ye'll *climb* like a wee spider, that's for sure! So on ye go. Ye know...what...ye...have...tae...do."

The little man's voice slowly faded away in Mike's ears; or perhaps in his mind? But he was no longer sure of anything! And suddenly dizzy, he started up the alley: at first loping, leaning into it, and then leaping, bounding, *almost* flying!

While high on the ridge of a sagging roof, the night-black silhouette that was Angus McGowan watched, guarded his thoughts and told himself: *Aye, go tae it. Get it done just as quick as ye like, Mike. For with a' that accelerant in ye—the red and the black and the yellow alike—yere time is verra nearly up. Perhaps six or seven minutes at best by mah reckonin', before a decade's decay descends upon ye...ye poor, dumb bastard! Aye, for they Francezcis allow but one warnin', and that's yere lot!*

With which he merged with the night and was gone...

But Mike Milazzo neither saw nor heard any of that. He was there beneath Kate's window; he reached up his bone-dry fingers and found purchase in the rotten brickwork where ancient mortar had fallen away from the curve of the arch. And from then on it was easy: He flowed or slid aloft, came to young Kate's window, thrust the curtain aside and went in head foremost.

The room was Kate's tiny bathroom. As Mike got to his feet a fresh wave of dizziness struck him; staggering, he flung out an arm and sent various toiletries clattering from a shelf!

Beyond the bathroom door Kate sat in a dressing-gown watching a late night show. On hearing the sound of falling objects from the bathroom she frowned, stood up from the couch, went to the bathroom door. The night breeze had obviously strengthened; now she would have to close the window.

But as she reached the door it was hurled open on her. Kate was thrown backwards; she toppled, her head striking the corner of a table. And with the smallest cry she crumpled to the floor unconscious...

XII

Only minutes earlier:

In the metaphysical Möbius Continuum, the Necroscope Harry Keogh had passed through a future-time door and let himself be drawn along the time stream. There the almost angelic chorus—that orchestrated interminable *Ahhhhhhhhhh!,* which sounded only in Harry's mind—somehow seemed reversed. He could only liken it to a red shift, perhaps that of time itself! Previously when he had fought against the *past*-time stream, the imaginary sound had been blue-shifted, higher pitched; while here in the *future*-time stream it was in the red, and would remain so until he had caught up with and was travelling as fast or faster than life.

Except that didn't happen; because before Harry knew it—and paradoxically unexpectedly, for it was the reason he was here—a crimson life-thread, or maybe even two, had angled into view some small distance away on the perimeter of his arc of vision. Harry had been scanning the future in every possible direction, because of which his gaze had at first skipped this crimson intrusion much like a proofreader skipping past a misprint before it can make an impression upon his awareness...only to return to the error as soon as his brain has accepted the message. And now, as he scanned that region of the time stream again—

—Yes, there it was: the crimson thread! (But only one now, which left Harry wondering if perhaps he had experienced a momentary bout of double vision?) Putting that thought aside, however, he concentrated on the crimson thread where it sped parallel with the bright blue life-threads of humanity. For even in that briefest of brief moments of recognition and shock, so the vampire had angled closer, full of a hunter's stealthy intent!

Up ahead along the time-line, young Kate's pale pink thread raced blithely on, but the Necroscope was catching up—even as he caught up with future time! In another moment he sped parallel with Kate...but so did the crimson thread which was narrowing down the distance between: the *real* distance, in the *real* space-time continuum. And events were happening so quickly that even as Harry gazed in horror it seemed that the crimson thread was about to merge with the pink!

Harry's immediate, instinctive reaction was to make an exit from the future-time stream...which was something he couldn't do! He hadn't discovered how to materialize himself in the real past or future; he wasn't a time traveller in a physical sense; he didn't even know if it was possible! The only place where he *knew* he could transfer from Möbius time to the Möbius Continuum was at the **Now** where he had entered, back then just a few minutes ago. Which was okay, because back then there had still been "time!"

Reversing his course, Harry "heard" the ethereal, monotone *Ahhhhhhhhhh!* change, blue-shifting as he struggled to fight his way back against the chronological current, finally arriving at the **Now** where he immediately exited first from the time stream, then from the Möbius Continuum, onto the landing outside Kate's door...which was where he had been all along, if not at this point in time.

This return to young Kate's landing was simply a measure of Harry's discretion: his automatic caution where a friend's life was concerned. He was checking that during his time in the Möbius Continuum he had not somehow strayed or been diverted from his location of preference and necessity, the landing where he had started out, to some other far less useful coordinate.

Now, having at least satisfied himself in that respect, he tried the door, found it locked, and found himself at a loss to understand how the owner of the crimson thread proposed to make his entry. Oh, Harry had seen the creature's approach, its *apparent* proximity to young Kate's pale pink life-thread. in Möbius time—but just how closely did what he had witnessed correspond to an actual event in the future of the physical space-time universe? And anyway could he trust what he had seen? Hadn't it always been true that the future was a devious thing? Only time would tell—and very soon at that!—as that mysterious, misunderstood phenomenon known as "time" continued to narrow down. And with little of it left to spare, again the Necroscope conjured an amazing portal and returned to the Möbius Continuum.

There he sought out a future-time door, but this time held back from entering to position himself in the threshold, at the ever advancing **Now;** from where he could gaze into the widening, blue-streaming future and await the advent of the crimson life-thread...

IT WAS AS BEFORE.

It was *exactly* as before, because in other than a parachronistic sense there *was* no before; this was the precise chronological moment when Harry had spied what he had imagined to be two crimson life-threads on the periphery of his vision. And now as "before," this time as a result of his eagerness or anxiety, he once again skipped over and almost missed the initial sighting; only to recover from his lapse so very quickly that the crimson blur of the after-image was still fading on his retinas.

And here it came "again"—which of course it must, because this was time in reprise—that *single* sentient vampire thread, that immaterial Möbius reflection of a deadly three-dimensional source. Little more than a red streak speeding into the future, still the vampire thread seemed monstrously intent as it veered toward Kate's pale pink thread where it held steady beyond the future-time door's threshold; even as Kate herself held steady, immobile and at ease within her flat.

But before the crimson thread could angle closer yet, which Harry knew it would because it had—and vice versa!—it was time for him to act!

The Necroscope still couldn't fathom how this plague-bearing monster hoped to gain access to young Kate's accommodation. Knowing that her flatlet was located at a fair height above the alley's worn stone steps, he hadn't thought to examine the exterior wall for windows. Thus to his mind there was only one way in: up these stairs to this landing…and then through him!

However improbable—unless the diseased creature had somehow come by a key to the downstairs door—still this last had seemed a possibility that Harry must consider and plan for; and one which he believed he could handle. All he must do was avoid getting bitten or in some other way infected as he set his plan in motion—

—Which was why he was now trying his best not to throw up as he munched on a whole clove of garlic!

The seconds ticked by, while Harry's nerves stretched almost to breaking; because if the plague-bearing vampire was on its way, then where the hell was it? A pointless question, for of course the Necroscope *knew* where it was: the only place where it could be—out there in the alley even now!

Certainly, for that was how close this creature had come to its victim in Möbius time. Except…

…*No!* Harry corrected himself. This sick, crazed thing had managed to get—and must *right now* be getting—a great deal closer than that! Why, it had actually appeared on the point of *merging* with young Kate, which is to say touching her! But how?

At which moment there came a crashing sound from beyond the door, a small distressed cry in a feminine voice (Kate's voice, which Harry immediately recognized,) accompanied by the slightest tremor underfoot, as of some dead weight striking the floor within the flatlet! But God! Surely not a "dead" weight?

Then, with his spine tingling—as finally he accepted the reality of what he had considered an almost impossible invasion—the Necroscope frantically conjured a Möbius door…

No longer handsome but ugly, pockmarked, and very sick, the ex-mafioso thug—the vampire Mike Milazzo—stood over Kate where she had crashed to the floor in disarray. Her once white dressing gown, spotted scarlet from her cut scalp, had flown open to reveal her beautiful, naked, almost boyish body. But still Kate lived: Her breast rose and fell, and she moaned however feebly.

It had taken the vampire but a moment to cross the floor to the open bedroom door and satisfy himself that there was no one else in the flatlet; satisfied in that respect, yes, yet despondent to discover that the one he had hoped to find here was absent. B.J. Mirlu's lover—who, until tonight, was to have been Mike's sole means of surviving the true death—had ignored his challenge and was elsewhere. And despite that the threat of The Chemist's synthetic diseases had been removed (as Mike had been led to believe, however mistakenly) still he must find a way to deal with this elusive, cowardly Englishman or suffer the Francezci brothers' wrath when they or their thralls caught up with him.

That last, however, was a problem for the future; while for the moment...Mike stared at the pulse in young Kate's throat, shook purplish froth from his scabby, flaking lips, and lowered himself to one unsteady knee.

Unsteady, yes...he was weak...he had needs...the antidotes were working too slowly, or he was expecting too much of them too soon. And here on the floor this gorgeous young creature full of what he needed most if he would live out his undead life to its fullest extent!

Such were the monster's mazy, drifting, but mainly puzzled thoughts. Yes puzzled: that while his vampire tenacity and will seemed unallayed—except perhaps by some antibiotic fever that was making his head spin—where was Mike's physical strength? He had been close to the final moment, he knew that, but surely by now he had drawn at least partially back from the gulf? Maybe The Chemist's remedies needed boosting? If so, Mike knew how.

His twiggy fingers, parchment dry, reached to fondle Kate's small breasts; and his septic, drooling mouth yawned open as he lowered his head...

At which there occurred a sudden compression of atmosphere, a stirring of the air and a fluttering of various loose fabrics throughout the room—and a breathless voice from behind Mike, saying: "You bastard thing—*now* I've got you!"

A hand in Mike's collar, yanking him off balance! And as he recovered, staggered upright and whirled about, the foulness of someone's garlic breath in his face; which anyone but a vampire would surely find more acceptable than Mike's stench! And there in a half-crouch before him, the very man he was here to infect with The Chemist's poisons!

How had he come here?...Where from?...What had he meant by that ridiculous, yet apparently threatening utterance: "Now I've got you!"?

For on the contrary Mike had got him, and would now feed on him! But only a very little—only a sip or two—in the short term to infect, but in the long term to destroy, putting an end to far more than any mere Englishman!

These were the vampire's thoughts in those moments first of astonishment, then of glad recognition and deliverance! But—

Were The Chemist's synthetic poisons still active in Mike, despite that he'd taken the antidotes? Surely they must be; for the remedies, only recently introduced into his system, had not yet had time to fight off his afflictions. And now, before that battle commenced—before Mike was completely cured, no longer a carrier—he must introduce the nightmarish trio of diseases into Harry Keogh's system.

All of this passing through Mike's mind in barely a second, the first brief moment of recognition. Now for the transfusion. Just a drop or two of Keogh's life-blood, a mere sip; something sweet stolen away, and something hideous given in return. Then, with the Englishman thrust aside, the main course: drained from the neck of young Kate! That was how it would be...

Or perhaps not.

Ignoring as best possible Harry's garlic reek, Mike reached for his lapels to immobilise him, draw him closer and bite him. But something was amiss: Where was Mike's agility, the preternatural velocity of his vampiric reactions? Nowhere in evidence! His eyes, despite being sick and rheumy, observed all too easily and clearly the motion of claw hands that no longer seemed blurred by their own speed. Indeed those hands now appeared to be moving almost in slow-motion, or at best languidly!

But while this was how the vampire experienced the degradation of his mobility, not so the Necroscope.

To him Mike's speed remained incredible: an almost subliminal blur that might easily—and probably *would*—have caught him off guard and might even have finished him off; but only if Mike had been physically capable. However, where the creature's will and vampire tenacity remained intact, his physical components—the fibers of his organs and limbs—were no longer responsive, by no means reliable. For with The Chemist's accelerants working on Mike's systems like acid, they were rapidly breaking down, quite literally disintegrating.

Harry jerked himself back from Mike's damp-gleaming visage; and several of the vampire's flaky twig fingers—full of leprosy and as spongy as puffballs—went with him! Still grasping Harry's jacket as they broke off from Mike's quaking hands, the crumbling fingers at once lost their grip, and along with their blackened fingernails slid from the Necroscope's lapels like so many giant, desiccated caterpillars!

Mike watched, in horrified disbelief as other chunks of his hands and wrists—like a catabolic avalanche of withered flesh—parted from him of their own volition, apparently in sympathy with the initial severance. And:

"*What...?*" Mike croaked through a spray of purplish-yellow froth; from which—leery of coming into contact with even the smallest drop of the vampire's morbid liquids—the Necroscope galvanized his suddenly rubbery and uncooperative legs, forcing them to back him off more yet. At the same time, however, reaching Harry like a breath of fresh air through Mike's suffocating stench, came the realization that the monster was done for, his termination assured. With the hideous *reduction* that was taking place in him, it could scarcely be otherwise.

Moreover, as Harry strove to recover from the momentary or partial paralysis of shock that he had suffered at the sight of this, the initial stage of Mike's imminent collapse, he also realized how fortunate he was that his plan had not come entirely unstuck. Though he had known, of course, that the monster was a plague-bearer, he could never have guessed at the extent or virulence of his sicknesses; but in any case to have ventured here unarmed, unprotected except for a clove of garlic—

—The Necroscope now clearly saw that this had been an absolute folly for which his only excuse, and a puny one at that, was that he had hoped against hope that the threat against Kate was an empty one, sheer bluster on the part of a failed assailant. Well, it had *not* been a vain threat after all—not by any means—but it had been Mike's last throw; and he too now realized that he was finished.

"Bastards!" Mike croaked, choking as he coughed up lumps of purple, perforated lung, seething flesh and gluey foam. "Lousy, rotten—arghhh, ach, *arghhh!*—lying bastards!"

He made as if to spring at the Necroscope, only to discover there was nothing of energy in his legs; they were bending sideways at the knees, concertinaing, threatening to fold on him like rotten sticks!

And yet, even with his head wobbling frantically on a suddenly scrawny neck, and as his nose collapsed into the sinus cavity behind it, still Mike managed one stumbling step before his right leg gave way and sent him lurching off balance, pivoting, and finally falling. At which the Necroscope at once seized the opportunity, grabbed the collar of Mike's coat, and dragged him bodily through a Möbius door. Which was as well, perfect timing, because at that exact moment Kate had started moaning again and was trying to sit up. To Harry's relief she was still confused, concussed; she had seen nothing of him or his departure…

Floating in the darkness of the Continuum—in darkness absolute—Harry held a jerking, spastically twitching scarecrow figure at arm's length; a figure too traumatized for speech who nevertheless continued to *think* great gonging thoughts into the mathematical Möbius Continuum, where even thoughts have weight:

WHAT?…WHERE?…HOW? What the fuck *is happening to me?*

And the Necroscope answered him, thinking: *Whoever you are, it must surely be obvious…I mean, surely you can tell—you can sense, feel—smell* (Harry shuddered!)*—that you're dying?*

What? You mean they've actually poisoned and killed me? Not because I failed them, but because they were going to do it all along? Yeah, I guess I know that now. And what the hell—maybe I always *knew they'd whack me in the end! Yeah,* damn right *I've known it! But what the hell are you? And as for this place: Is this where you go when you do your thing and vanish like you do? Is this where you disappear to? Maybe you're dead, too, and this is where we all go in the end…*

As Mike deteriorated he had commenced to ramble, and now he continued: *Hey! How come you're helping the brothers? It's like you've helped them to kill me! The brothers, The Chemist—even that fucking midget! But why you, now that I'm done for anyway?*

And again:

Hey! I guess I'm confused, right? But you have no idea just how much this hurts! It hurts like…like hell! *So if this is death, how come I'm still hurting?*

No, this place isn't death, said Harry, hauling Mike behind him as he headed for coordinates which he knew of old. *It's not death, not yet, and I'm not helping anyone. Or at least not the ones you have in mind, who I don't even know. On the other hand, maybe I'm helping everyone: Every ordinary human being that is, and maybe you should be grateful!*

What was left of Mike's brain was finally succumbing, collapsing inside his skull. But still he said: *Grateful? You think that I…that I should be grateful…to you…for fucking* whacking *me!?*

And knowing that the vampire would sense it, the Necroscope nodded and answered: *Well, yes! And maybe you should even thank me. Because I can feel something of your pain and how bad it is for you. In fact in this place I'm trying to* avoid *feeling your pain! But my way, the way it will be with me, it will stop hurting, be over and done with, much faster. Which is why you might want to thank me…If not now, probably later.*

Your way? said Mike, completely delirious in his agony now, his mind evaporating. *I…should…what?…thank you?… Because your way…of killing me…is…faster?*

Very much so, Harry answered, exiting from the Möbius Continuum onto a golden Australian beach in brilliant sunlight, and taking the disintegrating vampire with him.

The beach, which appeared to extend almost endlessly north and south, or for many miles at the very least, and was backed inland by dry, windblown scrub, was as deserted as the Necroscope had supposed and hoped it would be. Nevertheless, as Harry backed away from what he had brought with him, he cast searching glances in all directions in order to satisfy himself that he and the other were quite alone.

And then for the sake of his health he felt obliged to back off again—to step even further back—well away from the hideousness that was taking place before him…

XIII

Harry had not lied when he said it would be much faster. Indeed Mike Milazzo's decomposition could scarcely have been faster or any more complete. For as the seething had ceased even the vampire's bones had been turning to chalk, crumbling into the blackened, ugly patch of once-golden sand that was all that remained of him. Now, too, since a swirl of dust-devils off the land had taken most of Mike's gut-wrenching, doubtless poisonous stench out to sea, the Necroscope was able to move in closer, kneeling and using a length of sandpapered driftwood like the blade of a bulldozer to heap a thick layer of pristine sand over the still simmering, lumpy, but mainly liquescent patch.

Harry performed this last act after picturing in his mind's eye some sadly mistaken opportunist seabird settling to what it supposed was a free meal...a sickening thought, even to a man such as Harry Keogh.

But then, still not satisfied—desiring to be utterly rid of the remains—the Necroscope left the beach via the Continuum, and returned in a little while using the same mathematical medium, with a five-gallon container half full of petrol.

Then Harry built a small funeral pyre of driftwood over the tainted area, doused the desiccated branches and tossed a flaming brand, and stood by watching until every last trace of this man whose name he hadn't known—at least not yet—was reduced to smoke and blackened sand…

And then there were questions Harry would like some answers to: questions only he could ever ask, because he must ask them of a dead creature. And here in the mundane world of men, as opposed to the intangible, eternal, entirely metaphysical Möbius Continuum, the Necroscope could ask his questions out loud while relying on his deadspeak for the answers.

"Can you hear me? Or has your pain shut everything out?"

The answer when it came was so very faint that Harry almost missed it: *No, the pain is gone now. And it's so very quiet, so very…very peaceful! I can't…can't remember, when things were ever so quiet and…and peaceful! I feel…I feel that I'm drifting…like smoke over a blue sea. Drifting and drifting. And you: you're disturbing the peace, the quiet. Oh yes, I can hear you. But I wish…I wish you would go away and leave me…leave me…alone…to drift so thin and so light…to mix and…and mingle?* (As if the word in itself was weird, unusual beyond words; which in this creature's case it probably was)…*And…mingle…with…the…air!*

And for a fact the vampire, or his greasy black smoke, had indeed gone drifting out to sea, and was even now mingling with the air! Had the monster actually experienced this, Harry wondered? Oh, the Necroscope had seen death a great many times, but could never be sure how it was viewed by the subject, the sufferer. Some accepted death almost at once… others never; some felt raging anger at their lot…others knew only peace, like this one. Perhaps it was possible that a Higher Power had taken pity on this being—this once *human* being—who had suffered agonies both mental and physical which, for however fleeting or lingering a period, must have seemed to last an eternity.

"Oh, I'll leave you alone in a little while," said the Necroscope. "But I helped you, and now maybe you can help me?"

Help you?…But how…how could I…help…you?…And why… why would I…why would I want to?

"Because I might be able to do something about these people who poisoned and murdered you, the ones who put those synthetic diseases into you."

People?…Poisoned?…Drifting and drifting…So very…very peaceful…But murdered?…Whacked?…Was I…?

Fainter with every passing moment, the creature's deadspeak was losing coherence, breaking up and expiring, as if intent on following his atoms into a merciful oblivion. But:

"Listen to me!" Harry cried aloud, alone on the beach with only a ghost, or the echo of one, to heed him. "I shall do what I can…perhaps I can even avenge you!" (And to himself: *Even if you don't deserve it.*) "I may be able to seek them out—" he gave it one last shot "—for surely your murderers are at least as sick as you are—or were!? At least in their minds…"

Yes, my murderers! said the other, suddenly awake, a shade sharper, darker; but only for a moment, then fading away again. *But who…who were…who were they?…I think…think I used to...used to know...But now...now I can't...caan't...caaan't speeeak!...Can't any looonger thiiiink!*—

—Followed by a total silence that might last forever.

"But you *must* think!" Harry shouted. And then, as he made a fist and punched the air: "*Yes!* That's it! Don't try to say it, *think* it! Don't tell me, *show* me! You spoke of 'brothers,' of a 'chemist' and a 'midget.' But who were they? Now show me—let me *see* them!"

It was as if the Necroscope had lanced a mental boil to let the poisons flow. Visions, some of them as indistinct as phantoms, others as vivid as life, flashed across the screen of his mind in fleeting succession.

The brothers: darkly enigmatic in a vast gloomy dwelling, a mansion of sorts high on a cliff. The memory, a reflection from a dead man's mind, was there for a moment and gone. Yet in that span of time however brief, the notion had transferred to Harry that despite having suffered the true death still this creature feared that these brothers, whoever they were, might follow him even here!

And the midget: small but sharp as a knife. His sly, rheumy eyes might be old, but his vision was bird-bright; he saw without being seen. The picture from the dead man's fragmented mind was to Harry dark as the Edinburgh night sky behind the castle; yet oddly enough the Necroscope fancied he might have seen that shape, that silhouette, somewhere before. But there was no time to study it: a passing memory at best, it was there and gone.

Only The Chemist showed as more than a flicker: this "half-crippled" man who was by no means disabled, in his house in the dark of the forest, by a gurgling stream in the forgotten foothills of a vast and sprawling range. Harry glimpsed this thaumaturge exactly as The Chemist's dead victim remembered or stylized him, the very thought of him:

with his test tubes, crucibles, and every kind of electrical and chemical device—so like the hunched mad scientists of so many fantasy fictions.

Moreover, the Necroscope saw the route that the vampire had taken to The Chemist's Balkans lair; and like a camera Harry's mind had recorded the coordinates of that sinister house, even as Mike's mind had registered them, however involuntarily, unknowingly, during his time there.

"But if I do catch up with this Chemist—"

'The'...Chemist, came a sighing correction, as the tarry last patch hissed, popped, and issued one last gasp of fetor.

"—then who shall I say sent me?"

Fast dispersing, that final puff of intolerable stench was drifting out to sea.

"Hello?" Harry called after it as if into the aether. "Are you there?" And after several long seconds, as he was about to give up hope of receiving a reply:

M—i—k—e...! came the answer, as from a distant star. And that was the end of that...

To Harry it felt as if the night's work had taken forever, but in Edinburgh it wasn't yet one o'clock in the morning. He went to his gaunt old house and called B.J. on the phone.

"Harry!" B.J. gasped on hearing his voice. "Young Kate was attacked, but—"

"I know," the Necroscope told her, before remembering that he really should *not* know. "Is she okay?"

"Yes, apparently. A crack on the head: a bump, a small cut. But how do you—"

"I disturbed him," again he cut her short, "scared him off, intercepted him leaving Kate's place. So you can stop worrying, B.J., for there won't be any more trouble from him."

For a moment there was silence. Then in that edgy, wondering, borderline suspicious tone of voice that he knew so well: "Now Harry, you listen to me—" But:

"—I'll stay at my old place tonight," he quickly told her, "and see you tomorrow in the bar." Then, before B.J. could call him 'mah wee man,' he dropped the handset into its cradle...

Harry called Darcy Clarke at home, and in his turn the Head of E-Branch spoke to the Night Duty Officer at the London H.Q. So that by the time Harry had made himself a pot of coffee, drank half of it and taken the Möbius route to the H.Q., the special materials he'd requested were waiting for him. Past events had more than guaranteed Darcy Clark's faith in the Necroscope.

Offering no explanation to the Duty Officer, Harry shouldered the four heavy satchels, took up a marksman's sniperscope rifle loaded with a single high-velocity bullet, then departed the way he had come—but not en route to Edinburgh...

In the night dark woods at that misty place in the Balkans, behind the bole of a fallen tree on a somewhat higher elevation than the wooden house—a vantage point with a clear view over the perimeter wall to the stoop and front entrance—the Necroscope dropped off his burden of satchels and deadly weapon. And making a Möbius jump down to a spot within the wall at the furthest corner of the building, he approached the stoop from the side and climbed its steps to the door.

Harry scarcely believed that in this place—in the Balkans in Bulgaria in the wee small hours—anyone would be awake; but just as well to surprise The Chemist, he supposed, catching him unawares, half asleep; and of course he must ensure that he had the right man. One glance should suffice, for the glimpses that Mike had shown him—of an old man with a head wrinkled like a walnut, an apparently semi-invalid figure with a walking-stick; yet in fact a sinister creature and sound as a bell—had fixed themselves indelibly in the Necroscope's mind.

Thus it was with a certain degree of trepidation that Harry rapped three times on the stout oak door with the old-fashioned iron knocker in the shape of a clenched fist, summoning whoever was within. But it was Harry himself who was taken by surprise; for The Chemist, who preferred the night, was very much awake!

In only six or seven seconds, abruptly and without warning, the heavy door swung inwards perhaps sixty degrees; and silhouetted in the faint glow of a hearth fire from somewhere within, hunched up in his invalid guise, there stood The Chemist, walking-stick and all! It could only be him.

"Eh, what?" he wheezed, his voice unsure, infirm as he himself seemed to be. "What is it? Who are you? What do you want?"

"I'm Harry Keogh," said his visitor. "And you are The Chemist. I promised someone I would come to see you."

The other's mouth fell open in shock and he jerked upright, or almost, only to crouch down again. And: "So then," The Chemist's voice was trembling now, if only a very little, and possibly in barely suppressed rage, "it seems you know me—but who sent you?"

"Ah!" said the Necroscope, smiling a thin humourless smile. "You mean that one!" And then, nodding knowingly: "His name was Mike!"

Now The Chemist jerked more fully upright, and letting fall his walking-stick reached behind the door for what was standing out of sight, in the corner there. For a single moment only, as he groped for and snatched up his double-barrelled shotgun, The Chemist took his eyes off the stranger.

And fumbling and cursing, finally finding the twin triggers with a gnarled forefinger, then shouldering the door more fully open…

…But what was this? There was no one there!

Beyond the high wall, across the way and one hundred feet or so up the wooded slope, the Necroscope at his vantage point looked out through fringing foliage, watching The Chemist come running down the steps from the stoop onto his gravel drive. The little man, no longer hunched or in any way infirm, swung himself left and right, searching this way and that, his weapon at the ready—to no avail. The distant hoot of an owl, and the milky drifting ground mist—and nothing else.

But there *had* been someone…or had he perhaps been drowsing, dreaming? No, ridiculous, impossible! The Chemist stamped his feet, making the gravel crunch. Someone had been here; someone who knew—or had known—that ignorant mafioso thug, Mike Milazzo. Someone who must be here still!

Holding his shotgun to the fore, moving silently, stealthily, The Chemist ran to the left side of the house, disappeared round the back, came into view on the right and hurried back to the stoop. And there in front of the house, finally baffled, he paused, looked left and right and stamped his feet again, then rushed inside.

And one after the other, all the lights in the house began to come on…

Harry knew that The Chemist was fully alert now, that he'd soon be watching the approaches to the house from inside; most likely from the windows behind a narrow balcony over the stoop. It would be almost impossible for someone on foot to get close without being seen.

But the Necroscope didn't go on foot, he simply went—

—Down to a shaded corner of the house, where he placed the first of his satchels under the raised oaken floor, then yanked on a cord to set the device working. And no time at all to jump to the next corner and repeat the process; then likewise at the rear of the structure; and finally back to his vantage point on the wooded slope, where he took up the rifle and waited...

A count of mere seconds, and the compounds in the incendiary satchels—a deadly mixture of thermite and a chemical used in armour-piercing shells to kill or disable tank crews—began working in earnest. Even at that distance, two hundred or more feet, the incandescent glare of expanding spheres of light and heat at the front corners of the house was so blindingly white that Harry felt obliged to protect his twenty-twenty vision by half-shuttering his eyes...which he would shortly require to be in good working order.

Then once again a count of seconds, no more than a handful, before the shadows at the rear of the dwelling were driven back by dazzling globes of light. While at the front: flames leaping higher, licking halfway to the eaves where timbers caught fire; and the corner areas already beginning to slump down into melting foundations. While across the way from the house the Necroscope adjusted his weapon's telescopic sights and lined them up on the sturdy oak door, the stoop, its steps, finally the central area in front of the entire blazing structure: the place to which The Chemist must descend in order to escape the impending inferno. And no sooner was

Harry satisfied with the target area and his arc of fire—as he leaned more comfortably against the bole of the fallen tree—than the door of the house was wrenched open!

Venting his rage in curses and screams that went unheard in the roar and crackle of the fires, The Chemist emerged from his doomed house onto a stoop lit now in a white, orange and yellow glare. Shielding his face from the blaze as he lurched this way and that, he aimed his weapon ahead but found no worthy target; and so astounded, so enraged by events was he that he failed to realize how he himself—his dark figure against a fire-bright backdrop—made an excellent target.

But Harry took his time, and it was only after The Chemist came staggering down from the steaming stoop—when he paused for a moment to shake a fist and his shotgun defiantly into the smoky night air—only then that the Necroscope applied pressure to the trigger, shooting his single bullet through the madman's heart...

The place was completely isolated; there was no one to observe or report the fire, and Harry felt safe to go back down to the house and drag The Chemist's body up onto the steps before the blaze could take hold on them. Then, backing off from the heat and billowing smoke as far as the perimeter wall, he stood and watched the mounting fire, until the building sagged and began to slump in upon itself.

And standing there as the first hint of dawn coloured the sky a pale orange beyond the wooded mountains, it struck Harry as ironic that The Chemist—who, according to Mike Milazzo's unspoken yet graphic deadspeak recollections, had lived by the generation and use of synthetic plagues and lethal chemicals—had died as a result of alchemies no less ravaging: namely the contents of the fire-bomb satchels, and the pinch of explosive black powder that propelled a high-velocity bullet…

A fortnight later, when things had quietened down somewhat and both B.J. in Edinburgh and Darcy Clarke in his London H.Q. had stopped trying to ask questions of the Necroscope—questions he sometimes partly answered, though more often not at all, by reason of the strictures which, paradoxically, they themselves had placed upon him—then Harry went back to the Balkans with questions of his own.

He returned there, hoping that in the interim things might also have quietened down for The Chemist: that by then he might have accepted the truth of his demise, and would be calm enough and even grateful enough to converse with the only one he could ever again speak to.

For apart from The Chemist's role in Mike Milazzo's condition and activities—the fact that he had infected him, making him a plague-bearer—there were others who were also involved, who might even be the prime movers in the plot against B.J. and her pack. Others such as "the brothers," so darkly enigmatic in their gloomy manse in the heights; and, as Mike had referred to him, "that fucking midget!"—whose fleeting outline or silhouette the Necroscope might well have seen before albeit briefly, like a trick of the light. This was the question he intended to ask of The Chemist: Who were these people?

But no, it was not to be. Perhaps at some point in the future Harry might learn something more of them, might come across these individuals—or them across him—but not now. For The Chemist, who in life was ever precariously balanced on the very rim of reason, had now slipped over the edge.

And as Harry approached the damp, black ashes of the dead man's house and probed the deadspeak aether, all he could hear, and faintly at that, was the mad laughter and unreasoning ranting of dispersing residual *materia*—all that remained of The Chemist, blown to Harry from afar on unforgiving winds.

As for the brothers Francezci:

In their gloomy apartments at Le Manse Madonie in Sicily, they "heard" their mutant father's call from deep below; heard his shriek of uttermost rage reverberating in their minds, and felt their bitter vampire blood run colder yet.

You have failed me! came the furious cry from that ancient dried out well they called "the pit." *And the dog-Lord's bitch—she lives! She lives and he will be up! RADU WILL BE UP!*

And the brothers knew that their father, the Old Ferenczy, would most likely be right, of course. Radu *would* be up! Which meant that now they must plan anew...

AUTHOR'S NOTE

As chronicled in the preceding pages, these adventures of Harry Keogh during a strange (or even stranger!) period of the Necroscope's life between the novels "Wamphyri" and "The Source" were originally intended for inclusion in a long work in two volumes previously published as, "The Lost Years" and, "The Lost Years, Volume II: Resurgence."

Some fourteen years ago, however, having jotted down five pages of crabbed notes—notes which were barely readable more recently, when following this hiatus I decided to complete the work—I realized that the inclusion or addition of what promised to be a fairly lengthy episode would not only detract from the saga's pace but would also create an unbalanced and probably unmanageable length in the work as originally conceived.

Thus this chapter of "The Lost Years" was in fact lost and remained unwritten until I promised my current publisher a vampire story—and at once found myself scrambling for ideas!—until I remembered the above mentioned notes. Now, having completed the episode as it appears here, I see that I was correct: Had it been included, this chapter's length would have thrown all sorts of spanners into those earlier works...

Finally, the observant reader, on comparing this work with the aforementioned volumes—which I should not advise—may notice several minor ambiguities in the chronology, sequences, and character descriptions; these as the result of my decision not to attempt to "fit it in," but simply to write a connected story.

However, should my reader's curiosity have been whetted by what he or she has read here: Regarding the Sicilian Francezcis and their Scottish "watcher," Angus McGowan—the possibility of their future collision with the Necroscope, Harry Keogh—I can only point out that just such a future lies fourteen years in *my* past, and offer directions to the nearest bookstore.

The requisite titles remain as mentioned in the first paragraph above...

Brian Lumley
Torquay, Devon
15th June 2009